CHAOS

JB TREPAGNIER

Chaos© 2021

All Rights Reserved. No part of this publication may be reproduced, stored in a retrieval system, or transmitted, in any form or by any means—by any electronic, mechanical, photocopying, recording, or otherwise, without prior written permission.

Edited by Cj8168

Map art by Abdur Roub

Illustrations by Nancy Afroditae

Cover by Hannah Stern-Jacob Designs

❀ Created with Vellum

CHAOS

The Library of the Profane has everything your black heart desires. But we don't just allow anyone to get a library card.

Need to summon a demon? Raise the dead? A clan of vampires bothering you? Do you like really nasty werewolf erotica? The Library of the Profane has all of that, but not everyone can handle its contents (some people can't handle their werewolf erotica). I've been a librarian here for five years, and when I say I killed to get this job, I'm not being facetious.

You can't check out our books. Some books are sentient and don't like it. We have rooms to perform the spells in, and we do have a copy machine (copies are extra). When a witch came in and said they needed to do a little necromancy, I didn't question it. They wouldn't have been given a library card if they were going to raise someone terrible. I helped with their necromancy because it's just my job as a librarian.

Except it wasn't an ordinary resurrection. It was the physical embodiment of Chaos. When he woke up, he saw me first, and now he's attached. Chaos personified is a *horrible* library guest, and he won't leave with the witch who raised him. He's constantly getting into things he's not supposed to, and he's really into the werewolf erotica.

It's not like I can let him out because the Library of the Profane is meant to contain Chaos. The rest of the world isn't. He's awful about keeping his identity secret, too. A warlock, a Hellhound, and a vampire know he's here, and they are bugging me to let Chaos have a little fun.

I just want a normal day of summoning demons, cursing people, and telling them to be quiet in my library. This is too much.

TO MY FAMILY

If the words "werewolf porn" in the blurb didn't put you off and you downloaded this anyway, here are some explicit trigger warnings. Read any further and you will find detailed descriptions of werewolf cock, and some things going down with a Hellhound's dick. Orgies will happen. For the sake of me actually being able to attend family functions with minimal awkwardness, you should probably return this book and never ask me what I'm working on again.

THE PROFANE WORLD

CHAPTER 1
RIPLEY

What the fuck was Dorian Gray doing in *my* library?! I don't mean that in an *oh, look. It's Dorian Gray, the prettiest man alive* kind of way. No, I mean Dorian Gray somehow convinced the board of the Library of the Profane to house his stupid painting instead of putting it where it would be secure in the Museum of the Profane. They also gave him a library card, despite the fact he wasn't even remotely supernatural!

Oh, and that little deal he struck with a demon for the painting that kept him pretty and gave him immortality? He didn't even do the work for it. He couldn't. People said that he'd seduced a witch to summon the demon, and she was the one who brokered the deal.

Dorian Gray seduced me, too. But I let him. He was just so pretty and famous. I wanted bragging rights for fucking him, but after I went there, I'd never tell a soul. That is... unless I was starting a hashtag *#doriangrayisshitinbed*. I'll bet that would go viral because I can't be the only one who went there only to be overwhelmingly disappointed.

Not only was he a shitty lay, but he also stole a spell out of my grimoire on his way out. It wasn't even a good one, but it was one his vain ass was capable of performing. It was an eye cream that one of my ancestors developed which was supposed to reduce fine lines.

He waltzed up to my desk like I'd never get that forty-five minutes of my life back, and stole it from me.

"Hi, Ripley," he said, trying to charm me.

Did he actually think I wanted seconds?! Would anyone after that? I had serious questions about what self-respecting witch would broker a deal with a demon for him, given what a selfish lover he was. He never went for my clit... not even *once*, like his cock was some kind of magical vibrator and it just being near my vagina was enough. I was so embarrassed I ever went there.

"Hi, Dorian. Wow, your eyes look great today."

If it were up to me, I'd boot him out of my library and ban him. The board just adored him because that book written about him was still being taught in schools. They gave *him*, of all people, a library card.

The Library of the Profane was the biggest supernatural library in the world. We had books on everything you could imagine. Some of the books here contained dangerous magic, and some books were sentient. There was a magical vetting process that had to take place before they allowed anyone to get a library card. Fuck, *my* vetting process to be the librarian here had been intense. I actually had to fight people for it magically, and people had died trying to get this job.

The only books in the Library of the Profane that Dorian could even use as a human would be in our extensive erotica section. Werewolf porn was super popular, which the board had eventually agreed to including because rich people with library cards donated more money with it on the shelves. Now, I can admit being into it too, but I've read some fucked up shit with shifter dick.

Dorian fluttered his eyelashes like a teenage girl. He didn't have the gall to comment on the fact that he'd stolen from me.

"Thank you. Do you have a section on primordial gods?"

I gestured to the bowl on my desk. I already knew what it was going to say, but it was protocol. Dorian sighed and picked up the athame. He pricked his finger and let his blood drip into the bowl. Blue script rose from the bowl, and I pretended to read it.

"You're cleared for that section. It's in the basement. I don't need to tell you we do not allow those books to leave the library, and that if any pages are missing, you'll be banned. There's a copy machine on the second floor. Copies are fifty cents a page."

I *would not* put it past him to rip out a page of any of the ancient tomes on the various gods, considering he'd defiled my grimoire by tearing a page out.

"Thanks, Ripley."

My familiar, Felix, jumped onto the table and head-butted my hand. Felix was an all-black, American shorthair that appeared to me when I was sixteen and spoke with a distinctly British accent. I never knew if he was just faking the accent to sound posher, but I'd never ask or correct him. Felix might be a cat, but he had one of those Alan Rickman voices that could sound sexy reading the phone book. I dug the accent. Sue me.

"Do you want me to go down there and watch him?"

"You don't want to take a nap like when he was tearing pages out my grimoire?"

"I might be a familiar, but I'm still a cat. I require a lot of sleep. You were in bed too, might I add."

"Preparing to kick him out of my apartment when he came back from the bathroom."

"Is it out of your system now? You should have learned your lesson about the pretty ones when you were at the Academy of the Profane. Do I need to remind you about Tony?"

I groaned.

"Please don't. I just want him out of my library. I don't trust him. That painting needs to be with my sister at the Museum of the Profane. What does he want with this library? And why is he researching gods? Go watch him so I can figure out how to get him banned."

"I don't trust him either, for the exact same reasons. He's up to something. I'll find out."

I scratched Felix behind his ears.

"Thanks, Felix."

The Library of the Profane was my sanctuary. I'd always been a book nerd, and I fought hard for this job. I had apartments inside the library that were pretty plush. I knew every single regular well, including their reading preferences, no matter how bizarre.

I didn't trust most people that made deals with demons, even if only in the pursuit of vanity like Dorian. I'd summoned demons for information only, and I often helped other people in the library if they had that level of clearance. Every sane person who dealt with demons knew they were just as tricky as the Fae when it came to deals. Sure, they'd give you precisely what you wanted, and they'd let you have it for a good long time. Except payment would eventually be due, and you'd always lose. I didn't want Dorian Gray anywhere near my library when a demon came to collect what was owed.

CHAPTER 2
RIPLEY

Minerva Krauss was my advanced curses professor at the Academy of the Profane. She was a hard ass and had refused to give me an A on any of my papers, no matter how long or how hard I worked on them. Still, I fucking adored that woman. She was a super talented witch who had written a ton of books in the Library of the Profane, both on cursing people and breaking curses.

She was also *super* into werewolf porn.

"Ripley, dear. Is it in yet?"

"Yes, and I saved you a copy. I had a chance to read it last night, and you are going to *love* it. I won't spoil it for you, but the pack dynamics are amazing in this one."

So yeah, you could say I bonded with my old curses teacher about a book series we both liked, and that she was a lot friendlier to me now compared to back at the Academy. At first I didn't peg her as being into this kind of fiction because she was this prim older lady who always had tea and stale cookies out during her office hours, and her collar was always starched and buttoned all the way up.

"We'll have to have tea in the alcove and discuss it when I'm finished, dear."

I slid the book out and handed it to her. I'd love to pick her brain about all the books she'd written on curses, but I didn't mind discussing werewolf erotica with her.

She was honestly one of the most brilliant professors I'd ever taken classes with, and I totally fan-girled when I found out I was in her class.

A total stranger walked into my library next. I didn't just have a problem with the pretty men. This guy was my type too. He was massive, tattooed, and dressed from head to toe in leather. I was dying to know if there were other piercings on his body that I couldn't see, besides the visible rings in his eyebrow and lip. I definitely would have noticed him if he'd been in before; and I definitely would have flirted.

"Hey, beautiful. Bram Knotley. How does one go about getting a library card here?"

"Hey, cutie. You cut your finger into that bowl, and magic tells me if you're worthy of a card. It'll also tell me which sections you're approved to look at."

"Just like that, huh? So, I guess there's no way of cheating your way into the Library of the Profane."

Not unless you're Dorian Gray.

"Nope. Care to give it a go?"

Most people just pricked their finger, the test only needed a drop of blood, but Bram dragged the athame across his entire palm and held his hand over the bowl. The blue text instantly floated up. What the fuck? Bram was a Hellhound. We didn't get a lot of those here. They mostly stayed in Hell unless they were on a job. What would a Hellhound want with my library?

The magical system here was foolproof and didn't lie. It *only* approved people who wouldn't abuse its contents. I think the only reason Dorian got approved was that he couldn't technically use any of the books in here because he had no magic.

The system approved Bram, granting him access to all areas. That was almost unheard of. Almost everyone had at least one place that was off-limits to them. It wasn't just because there were sections containing things they couldn't access because of their species, but also that some areas had weaknesses that weren't common knowledge which could be used if a magical species war broke out. Why was a Hellhound given unlimited access?

"Well, that's certainly unusual," I said, leaning back in my chair.

"Going to share it with the class?"

"We don't get a lot of Hellhounds in here."

"Well, that's just racist."

"That's not what I meant, and I wasn't finished! You're the first Hellhound I've ever seen in here. Not only have you been approved, but you've been granted access to all sections. You aren't intending on causing any trouble in my library... are you Bram?"

"With such a pretty librarian? I wouldn't dream of it. I know you librarians like to shush people and hate messes. I'll be clean and as quiet as a mouse."

This Hellhound was precisely the kind of flirt that always got me in trouble. The sex was always excellent, and they *never* called the next day if you wanted a repeat. But, even after Dorian, I just did not need a palate cleanser that badly. I had a trusty Hitachi Wand for that. Officially not going there, no matter how sexy he was and how much he flirted.

"I'll be watching you, Bram."

"Do I get my card now that it's official?"

I tapped the bowl with my pen, and it made a singing noise.

"Your blood is your official card."

Bram just chuckled.

"That's savage. Only a witch would design a system like that."

"Watch it, buddy. I'm a witch, and I can make your life very difficult."

Bram held up his hands.

"Man, I totally don't fuck with witches. When I had to collect payment from one, she did something to my cock before I got her. It took ages to reverse it."

"How's your cock now?" I purred.

Damnit, Ripley, we said we weren't doing this. Felix jumped on my desk and glared at Bram with his bright green eyes.

"You certainly have a type, Ripley. One day, you're going to get fired for sexually objectifying the wrong patron. This one won't complain for sure but knock it off."

Bram just winked at me.

"Pierced and totally ready for action."

Why wasn't I going there again? Oh, yeah. Because shit would get awkward in the library when he ghosted me afterward. I changed the subject.

"Is there a section you needed help finding?"

"Primordial gods."

Why the fuck was everyone so into that recently?

I gave him my well rehearsed spiel about the basement and copy machine and sent him on his way. When he was out of earshot, I turned to Felix.

"Follow him and find out why everyone is so interested in that recently."

"I'll follow him, but perhaps you need to be reading up on them yourself. Trouble is brewing. I can feel it in my whiskers."

It looked like I'd be spending my night in the library basement instead of with my Hitachi wand. Fuck.

CHAPTER 3
RIPLEY

Okay, the basement was a hot mess, but Felix assured me that was all thanks to Dorian and not Bram. Dorian had yanked all the books down and couldn't be bothered to put them back. Bram was poring through the same books Dorian was. Bram could have put the books back. Asshole. I didn't even have to guess who'd dog-eared pages of ancient tomes to come back and read them later.

Every culture in the world had its own versions of the primordial gods, and so there's a lot of overlap. As far as I knew, no one really worshipped them or paid tribute to them anymore. There were so many different religions between humans and the supernatural. Dorian was a human who liked to mingle with the supernatural. Why was he so interested in this?

As for Bram? He had to be here on a job. Hell never permitted their Hellhounds to leave unless it was work-related. Demons knew things about everything. If anyone had insight on the primordial gods, it would be a demon. Sometimes, I wondered if Hell had their own massive library like this. If Bram needed information, he could surely get it from a demon instead of mucking around my basement.

That still wasn't an excuse not to put the books back. I'll bet if Hell had a library, they were much meaner than I was about messes... and dog-earing books! Show some respect.

"Are you going to have a librarian meltdown, Ripley?" Felix asked.

"Do you see this shit? I could forgive not putting them back, since Dorian has been here every day reading, but defiling the book by folding the page to mark his place? What kind of savage does that?!"

"Can you ban him over that?"

"Only if his name wasn't Dorian Gray. Half the board is female, and Silvaria loves that book about him. Clearly, he didn't fuck any of them, or they wouldn't still be kissing his ass."

"Some people wouldn't know good sex if it had a nine-inch cock that vibrated. It's like they haven't experienced it with someone who knows what they are doing. That witch who helped make him immortal went back for seconds, and I just feel sorry for her if it's as bad as you constantly complain about."

"And what do you know about good sex? You're a cat, and your penis has barbs on it."

"I haven't always been a cat, Ripley. I had a perfectly nice penis that I knew how to use before I died and was reborn as your familiar."

Well, that solved the mystery of his British accent. Totally real and totally hot. I was glad Felix had appeared to me because I didn't just like hearing him speak. He was pretty fucking amazing and snarky as fuck.

"I hope your life isn't shitty being attached to me."

"You keep things interesting, even if you have horrible taste in men. Look at you. One man you fucked and the other you wanted to fuck made a mess in this basement and assaulted your books."

"But I *didn't* go there with Bram."

"Hush, Ripley. We both know you would have if you hadn't come down here and seen this."

Felix was right. He knew me better than I knew myself sometimes. Bram was sexy as fuck, and I eventually would have given in. But seeing him misbehave in my library? That was an instant turn off. I officially wasn't fucking Bram for good this time.

"Why do you think they are both so interested in primordial gods?"

"I think Bram is interested because Dorian is. Dorian's payment to the demon has to be due soon. He may have gotten a witch to do all the work for him, but I doubt she agreed to pay the price."

I started smoothing out all the dog ears and putting bookmarks between the pages.

"It would get Dorian out of the library, but I really don't want a Hellhound collecting payment for a demon here. It'll be noisy and make a mess."

"You're a ruthless bitch who is super anal about your librarian duties."

"You know how hard I worked to get this job. My parents are so proud I ended up here, and Ravyn ended up at the Museum. If we were triplets and one of us ended up teaching at the Academy, we'd dominate the Profane world."

"You're also not the humblest person on the planet."

"Hey! Ravyn and I were tied for graduating top of our class at the Academy of the Profane, and look at where we are working now. I'd say we've earned some bragging rights."

"Go to bed, Ripley. We aren't going to figure this out tonight. Give me more time to watch them. Maybe Bram has already taken care of Dorian, and they will both be out of your hair tomorrow."

No. Bram couldn't do anything to Dorian without his painting. And he hadn't tried to ask me to look at it yet. Children weren't allowed in the Library of the Profane for a reason. I did not need some fucked up adult games going on here.

CHAPTER 4
RIPLEY

Dorian and Bram disappeared from my library after that night. I didn't know if Bram got his payment without Dorian's painting, but I wasn't questioning it. I highly doubted Dorian was gone. I went into the vault his painting was in, and there he was. All the ugliness of the years he had lived were still there in the paint. I only knew the basics of the deal he'd made. They fictionalized most of the book about him, but I knew if Bram were here for Dorian, he would have destroyed the painting.

I was starting to think it was just a crazy conspiracy theory that Bram was here for Dorian. Dorian was a hedonist after all, so he probably had it in his head he wanted to look at gods but got bored. For all I knew, he was in another country, partying it up. I didn't take Bram for a Dorian Gray fanboy, but I also didn't know the first thing about Hellhounds.

My life went back to normal. My library went back to its regularly scheduled program. I helped a vampire clan look up laws to settle a territorial dispute that involved digging up some ancient maps. Some werewolves came in looking for a cure to aconite poisoning. That was nothing out of the ordinary, and I knew where the relevant books were.

I approved and denied several new members. My regulars came in like they always did. It had been several months, and I hadn't seen hide nor hair of Dorian or Bram. Honestly, I was a little grateful.

If Dorian had tried to dog-ear the pages of one of the sentient books, it would have bled everywhere. I put them out of my mind.

One day a new face came in. She was very timid and seemed afraid of me. Honestly, no one would hurt her if she didn't get approved for a library card. I never assumed someone didn't have one when speaking to them. Sometimes, people had one and didn't visit often; or they had one and lived in another country.

"What can I help you with?"

She leaned in like she didn't want anyone to hear.

"I need help with some necromancy."

I pointed to my bowl.

"You know the drill."

She pricked her finger, and the blue text floated up.

Hettie Quinn, a hedge witch. She had full access to the witch section and approval for my help with spells. Which was fortunate, she was going to need it, because necromancy required potent magic. There was nothing in her file saying she *couldn't* raise the dead.

"Do you have the body?"

I *loathed* performing necromancy. Corpses stunk, depending on how fresh they were. Some in the supernatural community didn't believe in embalming their dead, and it utterly reeked when they wanted to raise them.

"It's in my truck."

This bitch right here was just driving around with a dead body in her truck! She did realize we lived among humans, right? Human cops would throw your ass in jail so fast if you got caught with a corpse. I pinched the bridge of my nose with my fingers.

"Get it in here before you end up in jail. You do have someone to help bring it inside, don't you?"

Hettie squeaked and nodded.

"Bring it to the atrium. That's where spells are performed. I'll get everything set up."

She scurried away like a little mouse. What was this hedge witch doing performing necromancy? She was just so meek. I already knew I'd be doing all the work and channeling her. Still, who was I to judge? Maybe she'd just lost her lover.

I grabbed the bowl, black onyx, and athame from the cabinet. I tried not to roll my eyes when Hettie and her friends tried to wheel the box in. All of them were tiny hedge witches, struggling trying to maneuver a massive wooden box. I sighed. I knew my back was going to hurt tomorrow, but I still helped them wheel it to the center of the room.

"Okay, if you don't have a library card, get the fuck out of my library!"

All five of the other witches grumbled and left, leaving just Hettie and me. I pried the lid off the box and braced myself for the inevitable stench. This wasn't a fresh corpse. This was a mummified dead body wrapped in gray rags. I'd been a massive fan of those Mummy movies with Brendan Fraser. Technically,

Hettie was clear to raise the dead, but I wasn't dumb enough to help her without asking questions.

"Who is this?" I demanded, pointing at the mummy.

"Seth."

We were about to raise the dead. This *was not* the time to answer my questions in monosyllabic grunts. I was prepared and willing to boot her ass out of here so fast and have this mummy transferred to Ravyn at the Museum of the Profane, unless she got more cooperative.

"Seth... who? Where did you get this body?"

Hettie was nervous. There were beads of sweat forming on her upper lip, even though the library was always cold. The atrium was even colder because it was all stone with no windows. This didn't bode well for me helping her raise this corpse.

"He's one of my ancestors!" she squeaked.

"Then why are you so nervous, Hettie?"

"I got my library card a few years ago, but I've never really used it. I'm a hedge witch, so I don't do necromancy. I know I'm asking for a lot, but I really need your help. I know your kind likes to look down on us hedge witches."

Was that it? It certainly could be. Other witches and warlocks like me looked down on the hedge witches sometimes, that is true, but honestly? I'd seen more hedge witches approved for library cards than witches like me because they didn't intend to abuse that privilege. They just wanted to learn. It was odd that Hettie hadn't been back to the library, but I knew from experience many of the hedge witches were sweet and harmless.

"I don't. I'm sorry. Come here and get ready to hold my hand."

I placed the black onyx over the heart of the corpse. I sliced my palm with the athame and squeezed my blood over the stone. I held out my hand to her.

"Chant with me. *Silenis Demonim*. I'll be channeling you, and you'll strengthen me if you chant with me."

We chanted together, my voice rising in pitch and my breath quickening as Hettie's remained the same. It was like she wasn't even trying. My blood sizzled on the onyx stone as golden threads wrapped around the body. That wasn't normal. The ropes were usually blue. I wanted to stop then and there, but I knew better than anyone you just didn't stop in the middle of a necromancy spell, or you'd create a revenant. This *was not* her ancient dead uncle Seth. I was going to murder this hedge witch and ban her from my library.

The golden threads wrapped around the mummy and exploded in a blinding flash of light. The force of it flung me all the way across the atrium and slammed me against the wall. I shook my head to clear it just in time to see the mummy rise from the box.

He tore the bindings from his body. He was glorious, at least seven feet tall with golden bronze skin and long black hair. He was ripped with muscle, and his silver eyes landed on me.

"Who calls me, little witch? I must make you my wife at once."

Oh, shit. That was *definitely* not Uncle Seth.

CHAPTER 5
CHAOS

What a perfect specimen of witch. She had black hair that fell to her shoulders in a mess of curls and bright blue eyes. She was covered in tattoos and leather. Exactly my kind of witch. She figured out how to return me to my mortal coil. Oh, I was going to have so much fun as soon as I married and bedded her.

She glared at the insignificant little hedge witch who was blasted back when I rose again and flipped her the middle finger.

"That *is not* your Uncle Seth. You'd better find some honesty, and quickly, or I won't just ban you from my library. I'll curse the shit out of you!"

Oh, she was the perfect bride.

There must have been some trickery involved in raising me, but deception was everything when it came to me. She wouldn't have been able to do it unless she was powerful. I scratched my chin. Technically, the little hedge witch didn't totally deceive her.

"There was a time when I was known as Seth. Or

Set if you like. I'm not her uncle, though. My spawn would be far more powerful."

"Oh, shut up!" she yelled. Now, I was the recipient of her middle finger.

Yes, this was definitely my new wife. No one else would dare. How charming. We could remake the entire universe. The little hedge witch was stammering and thought she had some claim over me.

"It was me who raised you. I command you to come with me."

I snapped my fingers and turned her into a cockroach. Her voice irritated me, and she *was not* the one responsible for bringing me back. This magnificent vision in leather who just stomped on my new pet cockroach was. I don't do favors.

"Who the fuck are you?" my witch demanded.

I strode over to her and stood so close that I pressed my chest against hers. She was a tall, slim woman, but nowhere near my considerable height. She wasn't backing down from me either, even after she'd seen what I did to that hedge witch. I knew things had invariably changed since I last occupied a body and walked the Earth, but one thing never changed. People recognized my power and cowered. Except she didn't. Magnificent.

"I've been known by many names, little witch. Who are you?"

I was dying to know her name, and I honestly hadn't decided what I preferred to be called this time around. I quickly learned something about humans and supernatural beings as they started evolving. *Always* pick your name, or they would stick you with a shitty one. I was one of the first things created when this universe was born, and some civilizations had given me some elementary ass names.

"Ripley Bell. You're in *my* library, so you're going to tell me who you are and why I was tricked into raising you. That hedge witch lied and said you were her Uncle Seth."

"The Egyptians called me Seth. Talented people. Maybe we can go there on our honeymoon, and I'll show you anything still related to me."

She jammed her finger into my chest and tried to shove me away.

"I *am not* marrying you. You have a fat head and won't tell me who you are."

I growled and strode forward until I pressed her back against the wall. I caged her in with my arms and took in her scent—incense and books—so perfect, so mine.

"I am Chaos, Ripley Bell, and you will be my queen. Only a powerful witch could have brought me back to my old body, and frankly, you're beautiful. We will wed and have many sons."

She placed her hands on my chest and tried to shove me away, but I wasn't going anywhere. Why was she fighting this? When I was on Earth before, I only had to nod my head and women fell into my bed. Did this have something to do with her considering my head as not proportional to my body? My physical form was perfection incarnate, but I could shrink it if it pleased her.

"Well, *Chaos,* it doesn't work like that anymore. They allow women to have opinions about who they marry. Men have to work for it now instead of having women sold to them like property for them to abuse.

I'm not marrying *anyone* unless I love them, and I don't even know you!"

Oh. Well, that part was simple. I might be chaos, but most people loved me. I'd just romance her. As soon as I woke, I understood things would be different.

"What century is this? I've been off playing in the aether and not caring about this world since people were unkind enough to entomb my vessel. I'm sure it's been long enough to forgive them. I mean, you were kind enough to bring my body back."

"It's the twenty-first century, and they tricked me into bringing you back. Two men I don't trust were showing a lot of interest in primordial gods, and one of them has a history of getting witches to do his bidding. Why any self-respecting witch would give him the time of day after having him in their bed is beyond me, but someone wanted you back to use you for something."

The twenty-first century?! Wow. I'd been off in the aether for a long time. Gods can pout like children when we want to. I could have come back at any time, but it was an affront that supernaturals and humans had worked together so diligently to entomb me because they lacked the understanding to appreciate that chaos was a part of life. I wasn't even the one that caused their stupid war, but everyone wanted to blame me when the shit hit the fan.

I just tossed my hair over my shoulder and laughed. I wasn't the only one to abandon Earth for the aether. Our disinterest in this planet had turned people so ignorant.

"I was created well before this planet, Ripley Bell. There's not a single creation on this planet with the ability to do that. Though I would afford you the luxury of the illusion you could, as my wife."

"We *are not* getting married, buddy."

This witch was so amusing. I loved that she denied me right to my face. It was refreshing, invigorating.

I'd taken plenty of lovers, but never a wife, not even from among my fellow gods. Goddesses were just so high maintenance, and I'd never met any other woman I wanted to claim.

Ripley Bell was a challenge, and I loved it. She was powerful enough to pull me from the aether and restore my vessel. My god mojo seemed totally lost on her. She wasn't falling at my feet like literally every other woman on this planet I'd bedded before. In fact, I got the distinct feeling she was whole heartedly annoyed by this entire situation.

"I respect that, but I'm telling you this now. One day, you will fall in love with me and be my wife because I will earn it."

She just glared at me, snapped her fingers, and I was suddenly clothed. We'd had this entire conversation with me wearing the remnants of old rags.

She might be irritated with me now, but I saw her peeking.

CHAPTER 6
RIPLEY

What the fuck was I supposed to do with a primordial god?! Especially one that had just decided we were getting married. Why couldn't he just be Uncle Seth, and this be like every other necromancy spell I've ever helped out with? I blamed Dorian and Bram because I had a feeling that hedge witch didn't come up with this on her own. Were they working together?

I couldn't just kick a primordial god out of my library in the middle of the twenty-first century. If word got out that I released Chaos into the world, I wouldn't just lose my job. If he made a mess, I'd be the one to die for it. At least now he had some clothes on.

"Follow me," I snapped.

Felix was hot on my heels.

"You are so fucked. How do you plan on fixing this one?"

I had no idea. Two people had been in the basement researching primordial gods. I had two suspects. There was Dorian, who'd already had a witch summon a demon for him, and I wouldn't put it past him to try to get a god to do him a favor. Then there was Bram, and I knew the only reason he could be here was a job. I'd never met a hellhound, but I'd spoken to demons before. They were always plotting something.

Did I just bring back Chaos for Hell because they thought they could control him?

Whatever the reason I'd been dragged into this plot, I needed to make sure neither of those men got their hands on this god. My apartments in the library had two bedrooms, but I had plenty of spare rooms. I adored living alone, but I also loved not dying after releasing a primordial god. I could give up my second bedroom to keep him hidden.

"You can stay with me, but only if you pass the magical test for a library card."

I loved everything about the blood spells that vetted people for a card, and that one drop would tell me everything I needed to know about where they could and couldn't go. I had trusted that system, at least until a hedge witch tricked me. She should have had a huge *no necromancy* warning on her card. I just hoped it wouldn't work against me with this god because I had no idea what else to do with him if I couldn't keep him here.

"You have a nice castle. Are you a princess?" he asked.

"What? No. I work here. This is a library, not a castle. If the library doesn't let you have a card, I've got no idea what to do with you."

"You could break the rules, my witch."

I whirled around and poked him in the chest.

"I break the rules all the time *except* when it comes to this library. I don't care if you're a god. If our system says you can't go somewhere, you won't. You won't cause any chaos in my library, and you won't make a mess. If you read a book, you'll put it back in the condition you found it in."

I probably shouldn't be bossing fucking Chaos around. Especially since I'd just witnessed him turn Hettie into a cockroach for irritating him and show no sign of remorse after stomping on her when she tried to scurry off! The Library of the Profane was a sacred place full of ancient knowledge and dangerous magic. It *was not* the place to abuse the system and raise gods just because our system didn't forbid you from doing necromancy. Yeah, I was super pissed they had tricked me.

"I wouldn't dream of assaulting books or harming your library. I'm quite fond of books. I missed them in the aether."

Chaos just earned bonus points with me, but I still wasn't marrying him.

I led him to the main desk and the ornate copper bowl. I didn't have time for pleasantries. All of Hettie's hedge witch friends who'd helped her bring the body were going to realize she hadn't come back. They didn't have library cards, if they did they wouldn't have left when I kicked them out, but they could still make an appearance to check on her and see Chaos. That would get reported back to whoever orchestrated this. I didn't want a bunch of pissed off hedge witches in here because I stomped on their friend, and I certainly didn't want whoever found Chaos's body to know I succeeded.

I picked up the athame and thrust it at him.

"I need you to bleed into this bowl."

I would give it to this primordial god. I'd been bossing him around like this big, librarian bitch who had no reason to be afraid of him. I asked him to bleed for me with no explanation given, and he just did it. He never snapped at me or pulled some *do you know who I am* shit with me. He very well could have.

His blood sizzled violently in the bowl, and I was worried for a second that it was going to break it. This bowl had seen the blood of literally every supernatural species on the planet, but as far as I knew, a god had never applied for a library card.

"How much blood do you desire? My wounds heal, but I can cut deeper."

The blue script finally floated up from the bowl. Thank Lilith. It was terrible enough Chaos was here. If I broke this magic, I'd be in serious trouble.

The script on Chaos was massive. It showed every single name he'd ever been known as throughout history, and there were a lot. He was also approved and given access to every single area in the library. Even after Hettie and Bram, I still put a lot of faith in this system. The library didn't care who he was or how old. He wouldn't have been given a card or access to all areas if he was going to abuse anything in here.

"You don't need to bleed anymore. You're approved and can access all areas. I have apartments in the library. You can take my second bedroom. We must get you clothes. You're massive, so we'll have to go to specialty shops."

Chaos just chuckled.

"I can think an entire wardrobe into existence. You don't need to spend your money on me. I can also conjure entire feasts. You'll want for nothing."

Except for job security with Chaos living in my apartment.

"The bowl told me all the names people used to call you. Is there one you prefer?"

Chaos looked pensive. He scratched his chin.

"I haven't decided. I've loathed some of the names chosen for me. What's a powerful name in this century?"

Oh, Lilith! I could not be responsible for picking his name. I was a witch. Names had power to us. Witches could do a lot with a little blood, hair, and your name.

"Why don't you read through some books here and find one that calls to you?" I suggested.

He got up in my personal space again. I always felt super weird when he did that. There was something about him that drew me to him. He was massive and gorgeous. Getting involved with Chaos personified was precisely the kind of fucked up dating history I had, but we weren't talking about getting ghosted or a broken heart in this case. Chaos had just turned a hedge witch into a roach for being annoying. I was super attached to my human form and not in any hurry to become a cockroach. I so wasn't going there.

"I'd rather you had the honor of picking my name."

"Nope. No way. I need to consult my tarot cards. The fiction section is just over there. Why don't you hit up the books?"

"Of course. Your cards will tell you we are getting married, by the way."

They wouldn't. That wasn't how they worked. But I could get some guidance as to why people were going around tricking harmless librarians into raising primordial gods and what was in store.

I could feel it in my gut. There was some nasty shit headed my way, and this was just the beginning.

CHAPTER 7
RIPLEY

I read my tarot cards all the time. I read them for library patrons when asked. My parents taught my twin sister and I to do it when we were young. When we got accepted into the Academy of the Profane, we had the best teachers in the entire world, including some who taught classes to hone our tarot skills.

I'd *never* had this many major arcana cards in a single reading before, whether for me or someone else. Some major shit was brewing. Felix was leaning over my shoulder, watching.

"Are you going to tell him you drew The Lovers?"

"Fuuuuck no. I'm going to ignore it."

"And what did Professor Barclay say about picking and choosing cards?"

"I know what he said. I'm not going to ignore it forever. I need time to process it. It doesn't mean I'm going to marry him. I'm not going to tell him I drew it because he's already miserable about the whole wife thing."

"You've sampled just about every species in the supernatural world and one immortal human. Maybe you're fated to be with a god."

"Stop it, Felix, or I'll get you neutered. This is a hot mess.

What am I supposed to do with a primordial god who thinks he wants to marry me?! *Someone* wanted him back on Earth, and I doubt it was Hettie."

"You drew the Five of Swords. How do you know the hedge witches didn't too?"

"I have no doubt the Five of Swords has something to do with it, but Dorian and Bram were both researching primordial gods. I have a feeling they are the most likely suspects."

"You're just being racist against hedge witches. They are perfectly capable of tricking you into a little necromancy."

"No. Hettie wouldn't have been given a library card if she intended to abuse the system. Bram wouldn't have either. That leaves Dorian. We already know he enjoys manipulating witches. Hettie was probably harmless when she applied for her library card, then Dorian manipulated her."

"You're really holding it against him, being a selfish lover, you know."

"Stealing from me! Of all things! Don't forget ripping a page out of my grimoire. I'm angrier about that than the shitty lay."

"Dorian is a peacock. You don't even use that potion. We know he likes being pretty, or he wouldn't have made a deal with a demon."

"Stop making excuses for him. I didn't tell him about the contents of my grimoire, so he wouldn't have known it was in there unless he was snooping. Oh, my

Lilith. You know the type of spells in my grimoire. What if he stole the eye cream but also took cell phone photos of some of the more dangerous stuff?"

"I usually lock it away when I have company, but I didn't when he was over because he's human."

"You have nothing in there about raising gods, but your family has dabbled in some dark magic. It would probably be wise to keep this god close to you, just in case."

"Why are you so gung-ho about the god and me?"

"Because I'm tired of watching your miserable dating life, Ripley."

"Keep insulting me, and I'll make that vet appointment to snip off your kitty nuts."

Chaos came bounding over to my desk with a book. He slammed it down, and I realized the gravity of my mistake. I'd sent him over to our fiction section to pick a new name. The *only* fiction in the Library of the Profane was some pretty extreme erotica.

"I haven't picked a name yet, but werewolf sex is fascinating. Did you know their cocks—"

"Stop!" I yelled.

I knew all about shifter cock. I'd experienced it in my bed, and I also knew they exaggerated the knot in fiction. According to the popular erotica, it grew to a tree trunk's size and got everyone pregnant if the wolf was in love. People ate it up, even if it wasn't totally accurate. I just had to direct Chaos towards the werewolf porn to pick a name.

"I've fornicated with female wolves, but never males. When we are married, do you think you could find a male wolf to join us? I'd like to experience the knot."

I started choking on my tea. Chaos had to be the

weirdest guest ever to visit my library. I talked about these books' plot with several patrons, but *no one* asked me to get them a wolf to try. Most people who enjoyed these books liked reading about exaggerated shifter cock... but no one in their right mind actually wanted to experience a twenty-inch cock that got you pregnant.

Except for Chaos.

"Most shifters have the knot, but it's not like the fiction on these shelves."

"I still want to try one, but only with your permission."

"You don't need my permission, but this is the twenty-first century. You can't just go around demanding people have sex with you because you want to experiment! People will get offended. There are laws about that now."

Chaos just yawned.

"How boring. Before I left, all you needed was respect and a delightful house. People would beg me to take them to bed. I didn't need the law to protect me from them. If I didn't want to, I just told them no."

I got a little pissed off. I guess it didn't matter if you were some ancient god. Men totally didn't understand sexual harassment or why it bothered women.

"Okay, here's the thing, Mister Primordial God. Consent is a major thing. Women have the right to wear whatever the fuck they want without commentary from men. We don't *owe* you sex just because we are women. Demanding and asking for it is offensive. It's not okay with other men either. People just want to be able to enjoy going out, dressed however the fuck they want, without someone assuming they owe them sex just because they left the house."

Chaos had the decency to look properly chastised then, after I tore him a new one for every person out there who had ever been sexually harassed. Maybe it wasn't fair, but he needed to learn how things worked in the modern world because back in his day, women were regarded as less than property.

"Ripley, I've never forced myself on anyone. The only people I've ever taken to my bed were those who asked me. I didn't ask you when I woke up because I don't ask. I was a little offended I was standing there mostly naked, and *you* didn't offer to take me to your bed, and then you didn't immediately say yes when I offered to make you my wife. I've never asked a woman that question before, but anyone would jump at the chance back in my time. You're a strange witch. I think even in the twenty-first century, people would *want* to be married to a god, even if only to use me for my power."

"It's fucking weird to propose when neither of us knows each other though."

"Why? I can see all possibilities at once. You're a powerful witch and a hell of a woman. Every plausible scenario results in us being happy if you let me in."

"Except I *can't* do any of that. Tarot cards don't tell me everything. If you want me to, you have to earn it."

Chaos just smiled and tucked my hair behind my ear.

"Just because I'm a god doesn't mean I can't do that. It'll mean more that way. I'll be over there, reading more about werewolf sex. I think if you stick with your cards, you'll see we are meant to be together."

He just disappeared, leaving me with my mouth

wide open. My eyes went back to the Lover's card. What I should have been doing was grilling this god who could see all possibilities at once over what kind of shit was going to go down since someone made it a point to pull him from the aether.

Instead, I stared at the Lover's and wondered exactly what kind of shit I'd gotten myself into this time.

CHAPTER 8
GABRIEL

I kept staring down at the tarot cards, trying to figure out what they meant. Something huge was about to happen in my life. I have never drawn that many Major Arcana cards before, and I had The Lovers in this draw. I also drew the Five of Swords, which meant something bad was coming my way.

My family taught me tarot reading, and they taught me at my magical high school, but it wasn't like I could afford some fancy college, and they weren't exactly offering me scholarships either. I swear, if one of your relatives goes to the dark side, even five hundred years ago, the magical community shun their entire line forever. I worked my fucking ass off, and I should have had a free ride at any college of my choice, but when witches and warlocks went bad, they went *really bad*.

There was only one in my line that went dark, but the deal he'd made with a demon left a considerable impression on many people. As a result my entire family became magical outcasts. My parents had to work fucking *human* jobs because no one would hire them for the skills that came to them naturally.

I wasn't doing that. I wasn't slumming it with humans when I knew I had specific skills. My family grimoire was packed with useful spells, and not all of them were tainted by that deal. Sure, there was some dank, dark magic there, but even dark magic has its uses.

I was now the magical community's dirty little secret. I was a freelancer and a popular one. They wouldn't put me on the official payroll, and I couldn't be seen entering their big, fancy businesses. They had no problem meeting me in dirty pubs though and wiring money to my bank account off the books when they needed a job done. My work just couldn't be tied back to them.

Yeah, they all might shun my family to the world because of one disgraced relative centuries ago, but I knew the dirty secrets they kept. I knew who was cursing who in the background, who was stealing, who was manipulating territory wars so they could come out ahead. It was total shit. They'd ostracized my family because of one deal, and the only reason the same hadn't happened to them was because they hadn't gotten caught.

I used to have all these plans to expose them. I'd air out every single dirty secret in the magical community, but what would it accomplish? If I ever settled down and had children, they'd go through the exact same shit I did. Just because I'd gotten a bunch of people in trouble didn't mean it would change anyone's opinions about my family.

So, for now, I took their money and got rich.

I was between jobs and reading my tarot cards. Every witch and warlock worth their salt did frequent readings. I was in a hotel room in Moscow, getting ready to fly back home after a job. This particular deck was significant. It meant something, and I needed help.

My family wouldn't know about this. It was just a given now that none of us would go to college, so the coven took charge and taught us everything they knew. If I couldn't figure out what this reading meant, they wouldn't either.

None of these bitches I'd done jobs for would give me the time of day, let alone help me. I was going to have to change my flight and take a huge chance. There was one place with massive amounts of knowledge that was open to everyone, if you could pass their test.

None of my family even bothered applying for a library card at the Library of the Profane, but I needed to. The process of getting a card was pretty infamous. It involved blood, and there was no way to cheat.

It was worth a try. I had nothing to lose if I got denied. The Five of Swords was no joke when you drew The Lovers and that many Major Arcana.

I was going to apply for a library card. I needed access to some of the books on Tarot cards in the library. Hopefully, the fucking library itself wouldn't hold one relative's transgression five hundred years ago against me.

CHAPTER 9
CHAOS

I certainly, enjoyed this century. People had come a very long way, but in some ways they had seriously regressed. I wasn't just reading books and trying to come up with my new name. I was watching patrons in my witch's library.

Computers and cell phones were marvelous inventions. There were no computers in the library itself, but Ripley had one. The cell phones were supposed to be put on silent in the library. Ripley's fury was absolutely adorable if one went off despite the rules. I offered to turn them into rodents because it made her so angry, but she seemed satisfied with just kicking them out.

Still, I'd seen them on their phones. Ripley wanted things as quiet as possible in her library, so you had to whisper, or she'd give you this scathing look. I understood the no talking thing, but some people just sat there staring at the device in their hands, like they'd been put in a trance, even with all the beautiful books and the amazing architecture.

I could read books way faster than anyone on this

planet. The writers of these books must have been confused about how wolves had sex, because there were so many variations about what a werewolf cock could do. I was getting confused. I still hoped Ripley would invite one into our bed when we were married so I could experience it myself.

I was a god, but I was good at sharing. If Ripley wanted to sample the wolf, too, it would please me to watch.

I was spread out on one of the reading couches surrounded by books. Ripley hadn't taken me out of this library yet but, honestly, I didn't mind. Her familiar hopped up on the table and glared at me with his bright green eyes. I loved all animals... *except* cats.

I was there when animals were created. They were all given a purpose, except the cats. Cats killed for fun and were so aloof. I never understood why people revered them and regarded them almost as highly as gods. And in this century, you couldn't go anywhere on the computer without seeing a photo of someone's cat. I thought they were cute at first, and I liked their independent spirit, but they always seemed to hate me, and if I tried to domesticate one, they took pleasure in destroying my things.

I looked up from the book in my lap and glared at the black cat. If he was a familiar and allowed in this library, he was surely a tame cat. I wouldn't say I liked the way he was looking at me.

Another thing I enjoyed about this century was iced coffee and Oreo cookies. It wasn't just the regular Oreos that were good either. They made different flavors, and they made them double stuffed. It was quite brilliant.

Food wasn't allowed in the library, but Ripley allowed me my coffee and Oreos.

I considered that a huge win because she was a stickler about every other rule in the library. I got it. She took pride in this place, and she had every right to. I admired that about her. She also knew I could just wave my hand and disappear any mess I made. I never did, but I cleaned up all the same.

This fucking cat. He looked me dead in the eye as his paw came out and toppled all my cookies onto the floor. He assaulted my Oreos for no reason, and it wasn't like I could hurt her familiar without losing Ripley. I'd never hurt an animal, anyway.

Still, a lesson needed to be taught. One that wouldn't cause an ounce of pain but would remind him every day not to fuck with me. I flicked my wrist and hit him with a bit of magic. He let out this screeching yowl and bolted for Ripley.

That cat was going to rat me out, but it had to be done. It was funny. Even Ripley could admit that when she saw how I upgraded her familiar.

CHAPTER 10
RIPLEY

I could hear Felix's cry of distress from across the library. I asked him to check on Chaos for me because I was busy with two wolves who were asking for books on their pack's history. The whole ancestry craze with humans was also a thing in the supernatural community, and this was a common request now, but digging up specific books on packs, clans, or covens always took a lot of research.

I dropped what I was doing and took off running for the fiction section. I swear, if that god had hurt my cat, I would figure out how to get him back into the aether if it killed me. Felix met me in the middle and jumped straight into my arms. He was shaking in terror, but he didn't seem to have a mark on him.

I stomped over to Chaos' favorite couch and glared at him. He was just sprawled out on the sofa with a book in his lap, like he hadn't just terrorized my familiar.

"What did you do to Felix?" I demanded.

"He assaulted my cookies, so I taught him a lesson.

I didn't hurt him. I upgraded him. If you actually look at him, you'll see he's unharmed."

"He had the cookies stacked so precisely on the plate, like it was a work of art. I'm still a cat. I couldn't help it. I knocked them over."

I sighed and held him to my chest.

"You're lucky I even let you have those in here. Felix is a cat. Cats knock things off tables. You can't hurt my cat every time he knocks something over. He does that to me too."

Chaos just smirked at me.

"But I didn't hurt your cat. You haven't even looked."

I pulled Felix away from my chest and looked at him. Felix was always inky black, but now he had white fur on his face. White hair that was oddly in the shape of...

"Did you put *a cock* on my cat's face?!"

Felix wailed.

"Make him change me back! I cannot have my fur form a cock!"

Chaos was just smirking like he'd given both of us this enormous gift by putting a dick on my cat's face.

"I don't hurt animals, my witch, and I'd never hurt your familiar; but he needs to learn not to touch my things. Besides, I enjoy looking at him now. It's an upgrade."

"You're older than the universe. Grow up and take this cock off my cat's face!"

Chaos just frowned at me.

"You mean you don't find it amusing?"

I actually would have if it weren't Felix, and I was trying not to laugh that it *was* him. If you've never seen a cat look utterly mortified that it has a dick on its face, I can assure you it was fucking funny. Except I barely knew Chaos, and Felix had been with me for a long time, so in this matter, I was totally #teamfelix.

"He's sorry, and he won't mess with your stuff again. If he feels the urge to do something cat-like, he'll do it with my stuff."

"This cat means a lot to you, doesn't he," Chaos said, his face softening.

"He's my familiar. He's been with me since I was a teenager. He doesn't like this upgrade. I know he messed with your cookies, but will you please just change him back?"

Chaos just beamed back at me.

"I know the perfect upgrade!"

I was about to argue that Felix didn't need any more upgrades, and we both just wanted him to go back to a black cat when Felix suddenly felt like he weighed a million pounds. I couldn't help but drop him. My eyes flickered to Chaos, who was watching me like he was waiting for me to open a Solstice gift, then my gaze shifted to the floor.

I was expecting to see some horrifically mutated cat, but there was now a naked man on the floor of the erotica section in the middle of the Library of the Profane. Felix rose to his feet and appeared to be patting down his body to make sure he felt right.

Okay, human Felix was gorgeous. He was easily six foot two with ebony skin and long dreadlocks. He still had the same bright green eyes. I snapped my fingers and conjured him some clothes.

"Felix? Are you okay?"

He just shook his head.

"This is my body, Ripley. This is me when I was younger before I died!"

"You can turn back into the cat if you want, but you'll still have the dick on your face. I'm sorry, but I like looking at it," Chaos said.

Felix held up his palm and conjured a small flame.

"I still have my fucking magic. This is amazing."

I know Chaos did this because he thought he was giving me a gift. I was happy for Felix that he had a body again, except I'd just lost my familiar. He had a life before he died and came back as a cat. He would want to get back to it now that he could. I wouldn't stop him.

I smiled at him sadly and pulled him into a hug.

"I'm happy for you, Felix. I'll miss you."

He just frowned at me.

"I'm not going anywhere. Something major is happening, Ripley. I can protect you better like this. If I can still turn into the cat, then I can still spy in the library."

"What about your family?"

"I died a long time ago, Ripley. All my family is now dead. You're my family now. I'm not leaving."

I flung my arms around his neck and squeezed him. I looked past his shoulder to Chaos, who was just watching all of this unfold, a serene smile on his face. I had to give credit where credit was due. This was a tremendous gift, and Chaos did it because he thought it would make me happy.

It did, and Chaos got a few more bonus points with me.

CHAPTER II
FELIX

I couldn't believe I was whole again, all thanks to just a flick of his wrist. I had been a powerful warlock. Ripley was a hell of a witch, or I wouldn't have been allocated as her familiar. I'd seen Ripley and her twin sister Ravyn do some fantastic magic when they still lived at home and then again when they were roommates at the Academy of the Profane. Ravyn's familiar was a bat. Still, there wasn't a witch or warlock alive that could restore a familiar to their mortal form.

It irritated me the god took offense after I just acted like a cat with his fucking cookies and that he'd put a cock in my fur, but I had to thank him now... even if he left the dick there when I decided to shift back to a cat.

It was easy to shift into cat form, and painless, unlike the shifters. I just thought about it, and it happened. I thought it again, and I was back to my human form. I had one thing in common with the shifters, though. My clothes didn't change with me. I had to fight my way out of a pile of clothes when I turned into the cat, and I was nude when I switched back; and I caught Ripley peeking.

Ripley might be an anal-retentive librarian, but she'd always been a sexual person. She certainly didn't dress like the previous librarian here. I'd be willing to bet that librarian showered in a Victorian looking bathing suit because she didn't think you should ever be totally naked!

Not my Ripley. She lived in tight, black leather and didn't care about showing skin. She was probably the sexiest librarian in The Library of the Profane's history. She was also extremely good at her job. I knew she thought the whole Chaos thing was this massive fuck up on her part, but I knew it'd happened for a reason, even if we didn't know why yet.

She had been focusing on all the Major Arcana in her deck and the Five of Swords, but she drew the Three of Pentacles too. A team was forming, and I could see it clearly now. Chaos *made* me a part of the group the Three of Pentacles signaled by what he called an upgrade, just to please Ripley.

The Five of Swords said conflict was coming, but the Three of Pentacles signified teamwork. Ripley would have a team to fight alongside her. She already had a god, and now she had me, but I had a feeling more would be showing up as the days passed.

I needed to focus and watch in my cat form, because Ripley wouldn't be paying attention. She completely ignored the Three of Pentacles in her deck and was still trying to figure out the rest of the deck. Sure, the other cards were important, but she couldn't do this alone.

Someone wanted Chaos back in the mortal realm.

That would surely blow up in their face. I got the feeling no one could control that god, especially after seeing how offended he got over those Oreos, how he'd stuck that cock on my head and turned Hettie into a roach because he didn't like what she'd said to him. Honestly, the only thing controlling him right now was Ripley, because he had it in his head they were getting married.

I had hands now. I could access the books here without Ripley to turn the pages. I knew what I needed to do, and there was only one way to do it.

I knew Ripley better than anyone, anyone except her twin sister, Ravyn. She'd let me in the library if I changed into the cat, and I could still read over her shoulder, but I had a body now and I could do more than just give her advice and make snarky comment about her choice in men.

"I'm going to need a place to stay, and a library card," I said.

Ripley was still ogling me and checking me out. If I could count on her for one thing, it was sexually objectifying anything with a penis. She had restraint when it came to acting on it, but she had a healthy appreciation for the male form, and she had no problem telling anyone that. She also had this weird way of knowing who she could say shit like that to and not end up losing her job.

I could totally admit to being one of those vain fucks that liked it when someone like Ripley sat there staring at me like she wanted to rip all my clothes off and fuck me right in the middle of the werewolf porn section. Except she needed to focus. I waved my hand in front of her head.

"Earth to Ripley! My face is up here."

She shook her head.

"I'm sorry. I've always thought you had this thing going with your voice where you'd sound sexy reading the fucking phone book, and now you aren't a cat anymore. Your body matches your voice."

Chaos set his book down and reached for his remaining Oreos.

"I'm a little offended you didn't look at me the way you're looking at the cat. I'm a fucking god, and he licks his own testicles."

Ripley finally snapped her gaze away from me and tossed her hair over her shoulder.

"Oh, please. Even if you're a god, we all know if men could blow themselves, they would."

"I've never even considered the possibility," Chaos sniffed. "Women and men line up for the honor. If I'm in the aether, I can just think it, and my seed forms a new galaxy."

"Ew. Keep your sperm away from me," Ripley said, wrinkling her nose.

I got the feeling most people didn't insult Chaos to his face, and if they did, they didn't live long. Ripley was walking a fine line. This god had a massive ego problem, and he might think it was cute she didn't immediately agree to be his bride, but he didn't strike me as being a patient god.

He threw back his head and laughed.

"Only in the aether. In my vessel, we'll have powerful little demigods. You're not ready for that, not yet. The cat needs a bed and a library card."

That was... totally odd. I took him for being a jealous asshole if he couldn't even handle me toppling his Oreos. I thought he would regret giving me my body back and take it away when he saw Ripley checking me out so blatantly. She hadn't voiced it yet, but it was pretty obvious I would stay in her apartment.

"You'll stay with me, of course. I'll find a place to put you. Come to my desk so we can see if you get approved for a card."

WHEN I WAS STUCK as the cat, I slept on the pillow on the side of the bed she didn't occupy. Chaos hadn't tried barging into her bedroom, but he knew I was in there at night and he hadn't killed me, yet.

CHAPTER 12
RIPLEY

The two wolves looking for historical records on their pack were still waiting and seemed irritated that I ran away just because I heard my familiar in distress. The rest of the supernatural world didn't get familiars, not like witches and warlocks. They just *did not* understand the bond. Shifters looked down on familiars because they couldn't shift like them.

I was still trying to process Felix's new human form and dealing with two wolves throwing a tantrum because I hadn't been paying them enough attention.

"Do you know who we are, witch?" one of them growled impatiently, his eyes flashing amber. "You know which pack we asked you to look into. We're practically royalty. We could have your job with just a phone call."

Chaos must have exceptional hearing because he was at my desk in seconds.

"Are you threatening my witch?"

I've *never* seen a shifter back down from a fight,

even if they were outmatched and sure to lose. Chaos was massive, and he just gave off this vibe of power and danger.

Don't ask me why I kept poking him because he could easily kill me. Both wolves visibly paled and shrunk back. It was kind of beautiful.

"We wouldn't dream of it. We just got a little upset when she ran away when she was helping us."

Chaos got right in their personal space.

"She was running to me. Do you have a problem with that?"

"No... sir," the wolves stammered.

"Good. Maybe you can clear up some things I've been reading about wolves. Do your cocks really—"

I *did not* let him finish that sentence. I think everyone except Chaos was grateful I found the stack number for the books they needed and sent them on their way. Chaos just looked utterly confused as he watched them scurry away.

"Why did you do that, my witch? If it embarrassed them to answer, then they should take it up with the writers of those books I've been reading."

"House rule. No asking my library patrons questions about their dicks. Have you picked a name yet, or are you just engrossed in all the sex?"

"I'm doing both, but I don't like any of the names I've come across. It seems like names are being reused. People have the same name as someone who might have abused the name that was given to them. I need a name no one else has."

I got that, and it wasn't his arrogance speaking. Names were powerful, and I'd seen entire lines shunned because of one person. A family name could be tarnished in an instant because of the actions of one person.

Chaos might irritate the shit out of me sometimes, but he had good things about him too, even if he only did them to impress me. He was the only god walking the Earth as far as I knew. It made sense that he didn't want to share a name with anyone else.

"Maybe you could write down the names you like and combine them into a brand-new name that no one else has."

"That's an excellent idea. Handle the cat, my witch. I just didn't like how those wolves were speaking to you."

I could have handled the wolves. They might have been high up in the supernatural hierarchy, but they couldn't have gotten me fired. It would have taken something much more severe for that to happen. Librarian appointments here were for life, and the process for picking a new librarian was so convoluted, they wouldn't start it again just because some wolves thought I was rude to them.

Like the library cards, I'd had to submit my application with my blood. It wasn't an instant approval either. They took blood for an entire year until they had a group of ten possible applicants. I was given a battery of tests alone, and so was everyone else. If you failed a test, you were cut. After those tests, there was a final, ultimate test.

We were all locked in a warehouse full of dangerous magic. I thought the goal was to disarm it and whoever made the warehouse the safest at the end got the job, but I was wrong. People wanted the job bad enough that I wasn't just dealing with dangerous magical booby-traps. People were trying to kill me to get the job, and they fought dirty.

I didn't get the job because I was the last one standing and did the best. The other applicants killed someone, but I didn't.

I had the best battle magic teacher at the Academy of the Profane. I knocked them the fuck out and contained them so they couldn't hurt me.

That was what they wanted in a librarian. With everything stored in this library, they couldn't hire someone volatile enough to kill to get the job. I fought back because I didn't want to die, but I didn't do it dirty, and I didn't kill anyone.

I should have been mad about that test. I mean, sticking a bunch of potential librarians in a room to kill each other was fucked up. I wasn't. I did the right thing, and I *earned* this fucking job. I wouldn't fuck it up.

This meant Felix would have to apply for a library card if he was going to stay with me and have access to these books. I trusted him implicitly and would have given him access to everything if I could, but that wasn't up to me. Sometimes, the magical system here would give someone a card I thought was shady as fuck. Sometimes, I thought they would approve someone, and they were rejected. That was the whole point of the bowl and the blood. It could see things I couldn't.

Felix picked up the athame, and I was worried. He still had his warlock powers, but now he could shift into a cat whenever he wanted. There were no dual-natured supernaturals in the entire world. When supernaturals mixed, it was always a mixed bag as far as what powers their child would end up with. There was always something dominant that won out. Some of the fiction Chaos was so engrossed in featured hybrid supernaturals with two unique abilities, but that never happened in real life.

I could feel butterflies in my stomach as he cut his palm and let his blood drip into the bowl. It didn't sizzle like Chaos' blood, and the blue text rose up like usual. It didn't identify him as being dual-natured.

He was still classified as my familiar and given access to every single area in the library.

What was with that? The library rarely granted anyone access to all areas. I had a library card before I became the librarian, and I was given all access. They even commented in my interview that it was rare.

I needed to keep an eye on both Chaos and Felix. Not because I didn't trust them, but because of my tarot reading. Something major was coming, and it had to mean something that all three of us had been entrusted with access to all areas of the Library of the Profane.

I was still ignoring The Lovers and not even considering Chaos's proposal, but I did need to figure out why someone wanted Chaos back on Earth and why it involved my library and me.

CHAPTER 13
CHAOS

This new century was undoubtedly attractive. In a way, it was nice no one knew I was here except the people who tricked Ripley into raising me. As far as godhood went, people were endlessly blaming me for everything. Sure, I've caused my share of trouble when necessary, to balance the universe, but people blamed me for every little thing that went wrong. Like I cared about sending a storm to flood a primitive village that was so isolated, the people were practically inbred!

This was nice. I could spend my time in this beautiful library reading and trying to figure out how to woo a reluctant witch. I was trying to give her space and let her come to me, but eventually, she would need me to deal with what was coming. I couldn't see the future, per se, but I could see all possibilities for what was to come.

The person who wanted me back in the mortal realm had an axe to grind with someone. Several powerful people, to be exact. I could see all possibilities. When those two parties clashed in their last conflict, things would never be the same again. It was an uneven match, and someone thought to tip the scales by adding a god into the mix.

That was just stupid. My witch was angry she'd been tricked, and I wouldn't say I liked the idea someone thought I would be a weapon for them because they called me from the aether. I intended to get *very* creative with killing them when I found them. The nerve! In this century, people had the arrogance to match my fellow gods with none of the power to back it up.

I was alone in my bedroom, reading. I tried to give Ripley as much space as she needed. I am a patient god. I've been alive for a long time, long enough to see civilizations die. I could wait for a headstrong witch to fall in love with me.

I heard a knock on my door. No one ever knocked. I hoped it was Ripley instead of the damn cat. I stalked over to the door and flung it open. Ripley was standing there, and I broke into a huge grin when her gaze trailed down my naked chest.

"Yes, my witch?"

"Felix and I are watching a movie. We've got a junk food buffet. Why don't you join us? I got one of the new Oreo flavors. This one is maple."

"What is a movie, my witch?"

"Television, really. Felix and I enjoy watching Doctor Who. There's a new episode on tonight. We can start from the beginning, and I can show you the past seasons, but this *is not* an invitation to Netflix and Chill."

I just stood there, frowning. Not a single word of that made sense, but I was happy to be invited. Ripley saw my confusion and gave me a gentle smile.

"Do you like theatre, Chaos? They surely had that the last time you walked the Earth."

"Of course. I even wrote some plays in my day. I had an entire troupe of actors that lived in my estate. It was great fun to invite everyone for a performance on my property."

"Okay, so television and movies are a lot like theatre. Imagine if you liked a performance and could watch it exactly how you loved it repeatedly, down to the smallest detail. Special effects have come a long way, as well."

I felt my entire body light up. When I had a vessel before, there was nothing I enjoyed more than reading and live theatre, when I wasn't off causing trouble that is. And my witch had just invited me to watch a show with her. It was a start.

She was right about a few things. She didn't know me. She had every single right to tell me no, even if I didn't understand why. From what I'd seen of men in this century, I was a catch in comparison, even if I wasn't a god. I didn't know her well enough yet, and that was something I needed to do. I could see every possibility of a future with us together, and it was going to be glorious.

I needed to stop looking at the possibilities and focus on the present. I needed to learn every little thing about my witch. I knew she loved and cared for this library with the passion of some religious zealots I used to know. I also knew she cared for that stupid cat a lot.

I needed to learn everything about her because in

every possibility I saw of our future, war was coming, and I needed to protect her.

CHAPTER 14
RIPLEY

My living quarters took up the entire top floor of the Library of the Profane. Technically, I could have turned one of the other rooms on my floor into a bedroom, but I only chose two. It was way more space than one librarian could possibly need, and they told me I could do whatever I wanted to that floor.

The librarian before me was dull and had horrible taste in wallpaper. It was all shades of pink and very flowery. I ripped it all down and painted the walls black or purple. Most of the rooms I'd turned into playrooms. I set one aside for my bedroom and another for a guest room when my twin sister needed to come to the Library to research something for the Museum of the Profane, where she worked.

Chaos might not know it, but Felix knew damned well there were plenty of rooms on my floor to make a bedroom for him, but I still wanted him in my bedroom with me. He hadn't said a fucking thing about it either.

I led Chaos to my television room. I had a giant

movie screen in there to watch things on. The library paid exceptionally well, as it should, considering I almost died for this job. I had one of those massive sectionals brought in to sprawl out on and watch my big screen in comfort. There was plenty of room for the three of us, even if Chaos was massive.

I found out I had a total hard-on for British television and movies after Felix demanded to watch some. A new Doctor Who episode was always a significant event in my apartment, and now Felix could enjoy my junk food buffet instead of eating a can of tuna while we watched.

I hopped on the sectional and patted the empty spot next to me for Chaos to join us. Felix had chips and salsa in his lap and was going to town.

"This is so much better than tuna!" he moaned. "I'm never eating canned tuna ever again."

Chaos reached for the Oreos I bought him.

"Why would anyone do that to tuna? Oh! I think this is the best flavor yet."

Chaos and his Oreos. It was just so weird that he was so into them, but I fully intended on corrupting him and teaching him the ways of modern junk food. I grabbed the Cheetos and stuck them in his lap.

"Try these and tell me they aren't amazing."

Felix reached over and grabbed a handful.

"These weren't around the last time I was alive. I had to watch you eat all this food and rave about it, but you refused to let me have anything except tuna when we were in here watching things. Some of it smelled amazing, and some of it looked foul. Ripley, can you get me fish and chips, now that I'm not stuck as a cat?"

"I can," Chaos said. "I can get some for all of us. Where should I go?"

"A chippy in London, but we don't have the time for that. The episode is starting soon."

Chaos just chuckled.

"Maybe *you* don't have the time. I'm a god."

Chaos just snapped his fingers, and all three of us suddenly had a basket of fish and chips in our laps. He could be seriously useful, and I loved that he got this for Felix just because he wanted it. I didn't think he just did it because Chaos wanted to try it either. He was trying with Felix because Felix meant a lot to me.

"Oh, my Lilith. It's covered in vinegar, and he even got a saveloy," Felix moaned.

Chaos was already halfway finished with his.

"The cat has good taste in food."

"Eat up, Ripley. It's best when it's fresh and hot. The episode is about to start."

"Where are the actors?" Chaos asked, licking vinegar from his fingers.

"Watch the screen," I said, grabbing the remote.

I realized something. I was having *fun*. I was about to expose a primordial god to the wonders of British television, and all he had to do was snap his fingers to bring us all food from London. I was just dying to see how he'd react to television. I would never tell him this to his face, but I thought his reaction to our werewolf erotica was adorable. I got them out of there before he could finish, but I seriously wanted to see the looks on those asshole wolves' faces when he demanded to know the truth about their cocks!

Maybe I should get to know him better instead of just figuring out how to keep him hidden. He was undoubtedly trying, and he was being kind to Felix now. And he was just so fucking cute with his Oreos and iced coffee, mowing his way through the werewolf porn.

Chaos gasped when the screen lit up and then fell about laughing.

"This century is intriguing. You mean you can watch this *again* if you like it? Exactly as it is?"

Felix had been a little #teamchaos well before he got his body back and fish and chips delivered by magic. He seemed to be all aboard that train now.

"We should do a re-watch from the beginning so he can get the full experience."

I was okay with that. Chaos was here now because of me. He might be a god, but he still had feelings, or so I thought. I had been mean to him and treated him like this dirty little secret I didn't want getting out.

Chaos couldn't be contained. Stronger people than me had tried. I didn't have any hope of keeping this a secret. But I could be kinder to him, since he was at least trying, and I could get to know him now that I'd accidentally brought him back.

CHAPTER 15
GABRIEL

My familiar was a snake, and I pretty much gave zero shits about who feared them. I went everywhere with Orion draped across my shoulders. I was sure the librarian was going to be a fussy old biddy who shrieked when she saw him, but she couldn't kick me out because she was scared of Orion. She'd still have to let me apply for a library card. After that, it was just up to the magic.

I kicked the door open and strolled right up to the main desk. There was a huge, ornate golden bowl in the center, and a stack of tarot cards. I didn't see the librarian, just a scorchingly sexy woman decked out in tight black leather.

"Where's the librarian?" I growled.

She just leaned back in her chair and looked at me coolly. I *did not* have time for this.

"You're looking at her."

"Way to go, dumbass," Orion hissed. *"You hate people judging you because of your family name and that ridicu-*

lous bun you insist on wearing on your head, and you just assumed the librarian can't be hot."

I knew exactly how to fix this. I was a bitter asshole, but I could turn on the charm when needed. I rested my hands on the table and looked down at her.

"Sorry. I wasn't expecting the librarian here to be beautiful like you."

"So... you either don't have a library card, or you haven't been in since I got hired."

"I'm here to apply for a card."

"Do you know how this works? Your blood goes into the bowl, and it'll tell me if you're approved and, if so, for what areas. If you're denied, the magic here will physically remove you from the library."

Well, that was a bitch, and probably painful; but I wanted this library card, and it wasn't just because of that tarot deck I drew. My college education was stolen from me because of my family's past. I *wanted* access to these books so I could learn things I had every right to know.

I knew it was a long shot, but I had to try. I grabbed the athame and slashed my palm. The librarian was just staring and frowning.

"What the actual fuck is going on around here?" she muttered.

"I haven't been escorted out of the building by magic. Is that coming, or did I pass?"

"You were approved, and you have access to all areas."

She was frowning like she didn't think I deserved it, and I was just done taking crap about my last name. Clearly, I'd done something right because I got approved for this fucking library card.

"You don't have to be a bitch to me because of my last name. It was five hundred years ago."

"What? No. I think the level of shunning that goes on in the magical community is fucking stupid. It's just super rare that anyone gets approved for all areas, especially witches and warlocks. When I got hired, they commented it was rare for me to have unrestricted access, and I rarely see it when people apply. It seems to have been happening a lot lately, and I don't know why. You must be a hell of a warlock."

Well, shit. That had to mean something, but I didn't know what. This was the least judgmental witch I'd ever met in my entire life. I was sure the magic in the bowl would have told her my family name. She didn't care, and she even complimented me.

"I need books on tarot," I said.

"We have a ton of books on that topic, or I can read your cards and see if it gives clarity to the reading you had."

I was sure this witch had the best education in the world. It wouldn't shock me if she were an Academy of the Profane graduate. Profane, Massachusetts, was better known as Salem to the rest of the world. The supernaturals called it Profane because of the atrocities that had been perpetrated against witches there. They reclaimed it and established the Profane world. The library, the museum, and the Academy were all here.

Still, it wouldn't hurt to have her try. I needed all the help I could get. I could just feel it in my gut that the spread I'd read was significant. I stuck my hand out. She could take it, or she could look down her nose at me. I didn't care.

"Gabriel Morningstar. I'd be happy to help."

Oh! That was new. She knew my last name, and she slipped her hand into mine despite that. She gave me a coy smile.

"Ripley Bell."

I was about to say something when an absolutely enormous man was up in my face sniffing me. I usually would have punched anyone in the face and cursed them for that, but I just got this vibe off him that told me he was dangerous.

"Um, Ripley?" I asked as his intense silver eyes bore into mine.

He placed his hand on my head and inhaled. I couldn't help it. I didn't want to, but I fell to my knees. What the fuck was going on? She wasn't kicking him out of the library. She was looking at me curiously.

"This one is important. Keep him close," he muttered, before leaving as quickly as he'd appeared.

Ripley was looking at me in total awe. What just happened? She helped me to my feet.

"Come with me. I have a feeling this will be the most important tarot reading I've ever done."

All I could think was *what.the.fuck* as I followed her through the library.

CHAPTER 16
RIPLEY

Did Gabriel think all the venom thrown at his family was because of something that happened five hundred years ago? It was way longer than that. I could show him some books on the Morningstar name. Yes, *that* Morningstar. Gabriel was a descendant of Lucifer Morningstar. I wondered if he knew that.

He certainly looked like one of his ancestors was an angel. He had his long blond hair pulled back into a bun, and he had these fantastic, crystal clear green eyes. I didn't know what Chaos was doing when he came over, but he was a god. If he said Gabriel was important, then I believed him.

I left Felix at my desk in case someone needed help and brought Gabriel to the scrying room. I didn't always read cards in here, I just had this feeling that if he'd come all the way here with his family history just because of a spread, then it was going to be important.

I waved my hand and lit the candles and incense in the room. His familiar was coiled around his neck with its tongue flickering out, sniffing the air. The snake was pure white with red eyes. I wasn't afraid of snakes at all and thought it was beautiful.

"Your familiar is lovely."

Gabriel held out his hand so the snake could wrap around his wrist.

"Thanks, but you are going to give Orion a fat head."

"Felix already has one."

While we were watching Doctor Who, Felix started purring in his human form while enjoying his fish and chips and then later again when he fell asleep on the sectional. It was adorable as fuck, and I don't even think he realized he was doing it.

The library had its own deck of cards, but I preferred my own. Mine were designed by a witch who had an ancestor that apprenticed under Botticelli and passed the knowledge down through their coven. It was gorgeous, and it just felt right in my hands. I pulled them out of the black velvet bag and handed them to him.

"Cut the deck. What is your question?"

I watched him shuffle the cards like an expert.

"I had a weird spread. I asked if my career path was going to change."

I nodded and took the cards back from him. I centered myself and flipped the cards face up. This wasn't right. This was so wrong. Gabriel and I were both frowning at the spread.

"That's exactly what I drew," he said.

The problem was, I'd drawn the exact same spread when I was trying to figure out what to do with Chaos. That just *did not* happen. Pretty much ever. Chaos was right. I needed to keep Gabriel close to me because something was happening.

"Where are you staying?" I asked.

"Around. Why?"

"Because I don't know what it means, but I drew this exact same spread for myself. That big guy that said I should keep you close? He's kind of important, and I believe him. I have an apartment on the top floor. I can turn one room into a bedroom for you. I realize we hardly know each other, but something is happening, and I think we are supposed to stick together."

It was a long shot, and I was probably coming off as super weird and awkward right now. I didn't know if Gabriel was in danger, or if he was supposed to help protect the library or something else entirely. I just knew I could feel it in my gut that he was supposed to stay here, and the library approved him for all areas. I could use as many eyes as possible.

Gabriel cocked his head to the side like he was listening to Orion. I really hoped that the snake had my back.

"I agree. I don't know what's coming, but this means something. I'll stay, but I like my privacy. Who is the guy who sniffed me and wanted me to stay?"

I wanted to keep him a secret, but I somehow felt I could trust Gabriel.

"I accidentally raised the primordial god, Chaos. That's him."

Gabriel just cocked an eyebrow at me.

"You'll have to tell me that story over a beer."

CHAPTER 17
RIPLEY

I showed Gabriel to one of the rooms with minimal shit in it. I waved my hand and conjured a bed. I showed him where the kitchen and television were, but we both wanted to get back to work. Gabriel wanted to hit the books, and I wanted to grill Chaos and Felix about that spread and why exactly Chaos thought I needed Gabriel close.

We parted ways, and I went back to my desk. This was a quiet time for the library. No major holidays or catastrophic moons were coming, and Mercury wasn't in retrograde. I had helped most of the people here today the day before, so they already knew where to go.

Chaos had pulled a chair up to my desk and was laughing with Felix. That was new. I didn't think he cared for my familiar. Felix now kept clothes stashed all over the library. He changed back into a man and was sitting at my desk. I wasn't angry about it at all. I could use his help.

"I'm glad to see you two getting along," I said, taking my seat.

Chaos smacked Felix on the back so hard that he nearly face planted on my desk.

"I like the cat. I've almost forgotten he assaulted my cookies. I've decided on a name!" he announced.

"Oh?"

"I want to be called Reyson. Reyson Discord. Felix says I need papers in this century, and they want to give me a number, like I'm a slave. I'm happy to hear that it is now illegal. I never liked it."

It sounded a little ridiculous, like a rock star or porn name, but it fit him. He seemed so proud of it, and I was happy for him. It'd take some getting used to though, because I'd become accustomed to calling him Chaos in my head.

"Reyson. I like it. It suits you. We should have a feast to celebrate you picking a name when I get off. Except we do have work to do. I need to figure out why that warlock and I keep drawing the same tarot cards for both of us. I've invited him to stay. He's taken one room in my apartment."

Felix let out a little hiss like he didn't like it, but nothing could ruin Reyson's mood.

"He's in your future, my witch. Yours too, cat. Mine as well. Fate has bound the three of us together. Something is coming."

"The Three of Pentacles," Felix gasped.

"What?"

"I told you not to pick and choose the cards when you drew that spread. You were so focused on the Major Arcana and the Five of Swords that you neglected the Three of Pentacles. You asked what to do about bloody Chaos when you drew the cards. It told you several things, but it also told you that you'd have help. You threw a wobbly over The Lovers instead of focusing on the full deck."

Reyson just winked at me.

"The Lovers? I told you."

I glared at Felix for letting that tidbit slip, but he was right. I'd flipped my shit when I got tricked into raising a god, and the first thing he did when he woke up was talk about us getting married, then I drew The Lovers. I didn't ignore it, though. I knew the whole spread was significant, but I needed time to figure out what everything meant.

"Well, Gabriel drew the exact same spread. He came here to apply for a library card to conduct research. I offered to do a reading for him, to see if it would clarify anything, and I drew it again. My question was what to do about Reyson. His question was about his life in general. He's a Morningstar."

Felix knew what that meant, but Reyson didn't seem to. I tried to explain.

"Gabriel is a descendent of a fallen angel. A pretty famous one. His family eventually earned respect, but one of his ancestors made a deal with a demon a long time ago and caused a lot of trouble. It's probably going to be another five hundred years before the magical community forgets about it. That family had it worse with the shunning because of the Morningstar name. I'm not sure if Gabriel knows all of that, since most people have forgotten."

"I know of angels. They are much younger than I am, but they were only just getting involved in Earth matters when I left for the aether."

"Lucifer lost the plot and tried to rebel," Felix said. "He got banished from wherever the angels live. He fell to Earth and sired a few children before he disappeared forever. Some people think he's off running Hell and wrangling the demons, and some people think they forgave him and went back home. No one knows for sure."

"Demons get really mad if you ask about him," I said.

"I'm familiar with demons, too," Reyson said. "Younger than me, but power-hungry little things that like meddling in matters they shouldn't. I used to get blamed for their antics all the time. Demons are not my favorite beings. I can tell you one thing for certain, they would not follow one man and make him king."

"Can we focus on my spread? We'll never figure out demons. All this is tracing back to you, Reyson. Someone wanted you back here, and now my tarot cards are acting up."

Reyson just tucked a curl behind my ear and smiled.

"I don't use cards to predict the future, but if one of those cards says you will have a team to fight what is coming, then you can count on me to be a part of it."

"What exactly is coming, and who thought you would help them if they brought you back?"

"Only a complete fool would think they could control me. But every possibility I see with you, and all these people that keep getting added, includes a major fight ahead of us. Several supernatural species will be involved, and it's going to draw the attention of the humans. They will join the fight, and many people will die."

"Unless we figure this out and stop them, right? We have this entire library, a warlock who used to be a familiar, a god, a descendent of an angel, and me. I already have two suspects."

Reyson just shrugged.

"Tell me who they are, and I'll kill them now. Problem solved."

"One is a Hellhound, and the other is only still alive because of a deal with a demon. If you kill the Hellhound, the demons will retaliate, and I don't think there is a way to kill Dorian with that deal. His painting is in the vault, but they might get upset over breaking their deal if we destroy it. We have to do this another way."

"Hettie came in with a bunch of other hedge witches," Felix said. "We don't know where Dorian or the Hellhound is. Whoever got the hedge witches to do their dirty work will wonder why they haven't brought Reyson back, and the other witches are going to wonder where Hettie is. Someone will come in here looking for her. I say we give them a little chaos in their lives. He can do that Jedi trick he did on the Morningstar guy."

Reyson just clapped his hands together loudly. Felix and I jumped.

"Anyone involved in my resurrection will now feel the pull to come visit this library. They won't be able to resist it, or it will do horrendous things to their digestion. Give it time. They will come."

Reyson was super handy in a pinch. I needed to do my part if we were to be a team. I might be a librarian, but I had specific skills. Minerva Krauss was a genius when it came to curses. She'd written several books on the subject that we had here in the library, and she taught me at the Academy.

She should be finishing that book soon and would then come back to discuss it with me over tea and cookies, in the alcove of course, where all that was allowed.

I needed to find out all the curses she knew that were too dangerous to put into print or teach to college students.

CHAPTER 18
RIPLEY

What the actual fuck was going on? Reyson put some sort of magic into the world to get anyone who might have been involved in his summoning to my library. I was expecting Dorian or Bram to show up, but when I went to unlock the door the next morning, an entire line was wrapped around the building. I'll admit to camping out and waiting in huge lines for the next Harry Potter book, but we didn't really get that at my library.

"Uh, Reyson?" I called, peeking out the door. I hadn't opened it because I didn't need that many people without library cards in here at once. Felix and Reyson were at my side at once. Gabriel was on book duty to see if he could find out more about our shared tarot reading.

"We are properly fucked if that many people are responsible for the god being here! Look at their auras. It's a mixed bag. It's not just hedge witches, there are witches and warlocks capable of dark magic, as well as some vampires and shifters out there, too," Felix said.

"You see auras, but I can see deeper than that," Reyson said. "They've all gotten into some dark shit. If I'm reading them correctly, every single being out there has been touched by a demon. I know you witches think you have a monopoly on making deals with demons, but back in my day, every culture had a way to do it. I doubt that knowledge has been lost.

"Even back then, that kind of thing was frowned upon. Some of my family preferred the aether to walking the Earth, but the ones with vessels had rules about the gifts we'd give out. We only meddled when it restored the balance. I will admit, we got out of control sometimes and let things go to our heads.

"Some of the things people petitioned us to grant were totally within our scope to give, but because we could see all probable outcomes, we saw what would happen if we agreed. Some of us did it anyway. I sometimes did too. People always want more than they have and will do anything to get it. I'm fairly certain it was demons who went around teaching the various summoning rituals, but they are out there, as is evident by all those people outside the library."

"Well, the two that were in here looking up primordial gods to make a deal, one was a human and the other a Hellhound. This all ties back to demons, and I don't know why. I don't exactly want to let all those people in here. If they've been tainted by a demon, then there's no way in fuck they've been approved for a library card. I don't like their auras either."

"I'll question them outside," Reyson said.

"No way," I said. "I get you're a god and everything, but all those people made deals with demons, and we know they wanted you here."

Reyson put his hand over his heart and fluttered his eyelashes at me.

"It's touching you're concerned for my safety, my witch."

Reyson flicked his wrist, and the entire crowd disappeared, except for one very confused looking vampire with an aura that didn't put me on edge.

"That one is genuinely just here for books. I wish you were less particular about your library because I could have saved one and tortured the information out of them."

Felix looked a little sick. He refused to catch mice when he was a cat, and I think he had a massive problem with torture. I did too, but I knew some potions that would have loosened their tongue.

"If more show up, save one. Don't torture them but bring them to the waiting area. There's a room I can sneak them in. Felix, can you brew a truth potion?"

"Bitch, I taught you how."

Reyson just growled.

"Watch how you talk to my witch."

"Calm your tits. That's just how we talk to each other. I didn't ask if you were capable, I meant could you go up to my potions room and start making one?"

"I know, but I had to deal with your difficult ass when I was stuck as the cat, and now it's time for a little payback."

I rolled my eyes as Felix sauntered off upstairs. He even flicked his dreadlocks over his shoulder on the way out. Ass. I turned to Reyson.

"More are coming, correct? We'll get one to question?

"It'll take them a while. Those were just the ones in driving distance."

That was *a lot* of people out there. More people than I ever thought had outstanding deals with demons and they were just the ones within driving distance.

We were so fucked.

CHAPTER 19
BALTHAZAR

What a fucked up day to apply for a library card. The line was wrapped around the building, and every single one of the fuckers had stinky blood. It wasn't like they took drugs or had an unhealthy diet like I avoided eating. It was almost like they all reeked of sulphur. It stank, and I was getting bad vibes off them. I was about to high tail it out of there because I just didn't do negative energy, and stinky blood was just about the worst thing you could do to a vampire like me when everyone just up and disappeared.

I was just standing there, alone, like a total asshole. I was about to jump on my Harley and get the fuck out of there. I didn't sign up for stinky blood and disappearing people. The fucking witch I had been dating turned into a psycho and started stalking me and blowing up my phone. I tried to break things off, and I even did it to her face instead of over text like I wanted. I didn't even ghost her.

Bitch cursed me anyway.

Witches stuck together. They wouldn't help you remove a curse without getting the story about why it was placed on you in the first place. Apparently, showing up at your workplace and threatening your female coworkers, and trying to hack into your phone to track you and read your text messages is not a sufficient reason to break up with someone, according to the witches at least. They all sided with my ex and so refused to help me.

I was desperate, so I headed to the Library of the Profane. Now, I had to ask myself if I wanted to keep asking witches for help or if I wanted to risk going in there. Yeah, I was going to nope right out of this property.

Until the doors flung open, and I saw the librarian. Holy shit, she was hot as hell. Why did the sexy ones always have to be witches? They always got me in so much trouble. And this one was a tall, slim drink of water with legs for days, all wrapped up in tight leather.

"Hi! Sorry about all that. Just a little bit of housekeeping. The library is open for business now. What can I help you with?"

"Well, darlin', I came to apply for a card, but if you're going to magic the stinky people away before you unlock the front door, I might be having second thoughts."

"Stinky people?"

"It reeked of sulphur out there."

"Interesting. You want to come in and apply? I don't bite."

I flashed my fangs at her.

"I do."

"No feeding in the library. House rule. Do you still want to come in?"

She seemed friendly, so I just nodded and followed her inside. The Library of the Profane was something else. It looked like a fairytale castle. It smelled amazing in there, and it wasn't just the witch. She smelled pretty fucking good too. She led me to a desk that was nestled between stacks of books and then pointed to an ornate copper bowl.

"You have to bleed into this."

"That standard for vampires, or everyone?"

"Everyone. If you want a card, you have to bleed for me."

"Kinky."

I grabbed the athame and slashed my palm. I could see the magic working as she stared pretty hard. She cocked an eyebrow at me.

"What did you say you're applying for a library card for?"

I cleared my throat. I took a chance applying here because I'd heard they based the system on magic. Even if the librarian were a witch, they would still have to help me on principle.

"I got cursed by a witch. I need help with that."

She didn't go straight to *well, what did you do to the witch* like everyone else I spoke to. She just nodded.

"I can help with that. Ripley Bell."

That was new. It was like she didn't even care what I'd done to another witch, which was nothing. I held out my hand and took hers.

"Balthazar Orsini. I have to tell you. No other witch has been willing to help me."

"Of *the* Orsini? Nice. Let me guess. They sided with

the witch, even if she was wrong. Why don't you tell me what happened?"

Could I have actually met a sane witch?! Or was I going to ruin everything when I told her about my ex? Something about her blood told me I could trust this woman. Her blood smelled like honeyed vanilla and old books.

"We were dating and—"

Ripley held up her hand.

"Say no more. Cursing your ex after you've graduated high school is just juvenile. Seriously. Grow up. I'll help you if you help me."

"Oh?"

"You got approved for all areas of the library, and that seldom happens, at least not until recently. I'm starting to think all these people getting approved is connected to a tarot card reading. I think you're important to something. I'll help remove your curse, but will you at least stick around and hear me out?"

I was about to say yes when a smell hit my nostrils. It was a potent, rich scent that smelled like earthy mahogany and teakwood. I'd *never* smelled blood like that before. I knew I'd help Ripley, but I needed to find the source of the scent.

I used my vampire speed to run towards the source. That was sheer power. What was Ripley hiding in this library?

CHAPTER 20
CHAOS

This would be so much easier if I could just squash a few insignificant supernatural heads, but my witch wanted to use magic. Apparently, people frowned on torture and murder in this century. I'm not sure why she was so against it now, considering that fact I witnessed her stomp on that hedge witch I turned into a roach.

The cat was hunched over a cauldron, stirring carefully and shooting me daggers. I'd never tell him this, but I found him amusing. I didn't particularly appreciate how he talked to my witch sometimes, but it seemed to be the relationship they had, and it didn't bother her.

We weren't late coming downstairs, per se, but the reason we hadn't seen the line forming around the building at dawn was that we had been up late. Ripley showed me her favorite movies, and we watched her Doctor Who show from the beginning.

Television was quite remarkable. Even with all my powers, if I enjoyed a theatre performance, I could replay it in my head exactly as it was, but I couldn't experience the magic of seeing it again with other people, feeding off their reactions. There were many things I didn't understand about this century, but there were many things I enjoyed.

Ripley suggested that, since I enjoyed the iced coffee she made for me every day, I should try something called a Frappuccino.

She told me where to find it, and I brought three of them in for us. Ripley seemed happy but the cat just scowled and called it an abomination. He said tea was by far superior. So, I stole his and drank it since the fucking feline couldn't appreciate coffee, sugar, ice, and whipped cream. And it was even better if you dipped the chocolate covered Oreos Ripley had gotten for me in it. My witch was full of marvelous ideas.

The cat peered up from the cauldron.

"Do you have to make those moaning noises when you eat? This is a delicate potion."

I chewed my Oreos even louder and let out a moan worthy of having a wench in my bed.

"You made similar noises with the fish and chips, Cat."

"My name is Felix. You made an enormous deal about picking your name. You could at least do me the courtesy of using mine. Like it or not, I come with Ripley."

I was aware; so was the warlock and probably a few others. The possibilities for her future kept changing as decisions were made. Yeah, I altered things when I gave the cat his body back, but I wasn't mad about it. The cat was just so uppity, and it amused me to annoy him.

"In more ways than you know, Felix."

"I'm not listening to you. If I don't get this next step exactly right, this potion is going to explode, and we'll have to get a motel room for the night."

"Is that like an inn?"

"Yeah, but they have cable now. The beds aren't nearly as comfortable as the beds here, and we won't have any access to Ripley's magic supplies. So, shut up."

I walked to Felix and peered over his shoulder. I was curious about why he was making some complicated potion that could kick us out of our home when I could get the answers with a touch. Of course it would liquefy the brain of the person I was questioning, but I had no problem doing that to bad people. I had no issues doing that to extremely irritating people either.

Felix was carefully stirring his potion counterclockwise. He reached into a jar and pulled out something that reeked like a drunkard's asshole. He dropped a pinch into the thick, black sludge in the cauldron, and it started violently hissing and smoking. There wasn't an unpleasant smell, and it didn't explode. I watched the potion change from sludge to a clear blue liquid.

"Nice!" I said, clapping him on the back. "I knew you could do it."

The cat looked entirely put out, but I *did not* compliment people unless I meant it. What was his problem? He'd been stuck as a cat too long. That had to be it.

"Do you have to wallop me when you do that? I almost ended up face first in this potion. It only takes one drop. It would have been catastrophic for me to end up with that much on my face."

Right. Humans and supernaturals were just so breakable compared to me. I thought I remembered just the right amount to touch people without breaking their entire body, but clearly, I'd overestimated. I didn't want to hurt the cat. He meant a lot to Ripley, and I would admit to enjoying having him around.

"I'm sorry, Felix. Sometimes, I forget my own strength. Do you need any help?"

"It's done. I just need to bottle it up. Can you go let Ripley know it's done and see if she needs any help?"

I could definitely do that. Things were going to get intense soon. I'd hardly started walking down the staircase to the first floor when I saw a vampire trying to rush me. To most people, they couldn't be seen when they were using their enhanced speed, but I could easily see them as if they were a human out for a lazy jog.

This was the same vampire I left outside the library because he wasn't tainted by demons. I knew that he wasn't up to no good, but I also knew my witch had a thing about prohibiting running in her library. I used my own unnatural speed to meet him on the second story and snatch him out of the air by his neck. His fangs were out, and he looked totally shocked to find that he was now dangling from my fist.

"No running in the library!" I barked.

He was gasping for air and clawing at my hand. Ripley finally caught up with us. She glared at both of us like I was the one in the wrong here. I was going to need to learn my witch's triggers about what was and wasn't acceptable in this library, because I thought I had just done her a favor.

"Reyson, put him down, please. Balthazar, what the fuck was that?"

I set the vampire on his feet and glared at him. I

allowed no one to upset my witch. The vampire gasped and rubbed his throat. He was looking at me instead of Ripley.

"What are you? I've *never* smelled blood like yours before, and I'm fighting the urge to kneel to you."

"I'm the g—"

Ripley cut me off.

"Remember when I said I think you are a part of this, and I need your help? I asked you to hear me out, not run all over my library like a bat out of hell!"

I placed my hand on his forehead and scanned for all possibilities. Ripley was right. His future was tied to Ripley's and mine. Now, I was glad I hadn't thrown him down the stairs. What all those demon tainted people had been doing outside the library and why, out of all my family, they chose to bring me back, this vampire was a part of it all somehow.

"He's part of the possibilities now," I said, releasing him.

"Someone had better start explaining, or I'm getting the fuck out of here. I'll find another way to deal with my curse."

"Long story short, some people involved with demons tricked me into doing some necromancy and restoring the primordial god, Chaos, back to his vessel. This is him, and he prefers to be called Reyson. Something big is coming, and I think the magic in the library is trying to tell me you're meant to help."

That was new. Ripley must have had a revelation when taking his blood for the library card.

"What makes you think a cursed vampire is going to be any help?"

"I know it sounds fucked up, but the library seldom

gives anyone access to every section here. It was rare when it gave it to me, and I haven't seen it happen again during the entire five years I've been a librarian here. It started with a Hellhound and started getting more frequent after Reyson came back. Reyson can tell by touching you, but I really think the library is trying to tell me something by handing out all-access library cards.

"Think about it. You're a vampire here to break a curse. Almost every other vampire would have been given access to the vampire and fiction sections, and I would have helped you break the curse. A lot of the books here are sentient, and so is the library itself. The library won't approve you if you intend to use its contents to cause harm. There are also other safeguards in place like restricting which sections people have access to, in case you change your mind or get corrupted later.

"When you give your blood as the library card, the library knows if you are asking for something you shouldn't. It'll revoke your library card and remove you from the library if you do. It *should* have done that with Hettie, that is unless the library thought Reyson should be here. I ran her blood, and it said they cleared her for necromancy. I was pissed she tricked me, but now I think it was never a trick. Those people may have wanted Reyson for something, but it was never in the cards for them. Now, he's on our side. He's part of the team."

I'd take that for now. I wasn't just helping because I could see Ripley was my match. I had caused some wars in my time because we needed it to restore balance. This fight that was coming was unnatural. It wasn't meant to happen. Many people thought I reveled in all forms of chaos, no matter who caused it, but that wasn't my purpose.

Sure, I totally loved causing it when it was needed, but it didn't need to happen all the time. I didn't just cause chaos randomly, and I punished the wicked who did it without my blessing.

Based on the number of people outside the library, many evil people needed to die.

CHAPTER 21
RIPLEY

My working theory that the library wanted Reyson here and that it was trying to help by granting all-access passes to certain people held true because Reyson could just touch someone and confirm it. He was becoming pretty handy to have around, even if he could be a horrible library guest, and he annoyed Felix.

What about Bram?

That was my primary question. He was the first patron in my five years here to be granted full access. He was also one of my prime suspects, but he couldn't be if the library vetting system was accurate. Though I had a million questions for him and I couldn't find him. I didn't know if Reyson's spell would draw Bram here because it might not involve him.

Still, I liked Bram more than I liked Dorian, but there were so many signs pointing towards him. Dorian, too for that matter. Why were there that many people outside the library who had made deals with demons when Reyson sent that magic out? And how many more would show up?

What did Hell want with Reyson? Demons were supposed to have all kinds of magic. If they wanted to summon a god forth, I was reasonably sure they could do that without me. I both suspected Bram and believed he was part of my team at the same time.

All signs pointed to Hell, but my library would have kicked him out if Hell was planning a war.

That left Dorian. I wasn't the one who tested his blood for the library card. Silvaria came in before the library was open and abused her board position to test him while I was sleeping. I never actually witnessed the test. I woke up and came down for work and Silvaria was sitting at my desk, shooting the shit with Dorian.

I didn't know how to cheat the blood test, but that doesn't mean it isn't possible, and that was the entire reason I had to deal with Dorian Gray in my library. Silvaria was one of those wealthy witches who always had affairs with her pool boys. Dorian would totally be her type, even if she didn't think that fucking book about him was the best thing ever written, and we should carry it in the library.

I had two plans in my head. One was to summon a demon and just ask. There was a particular demon I invoked when I wanted information that didn't exist on Earth. Arzareth. She was a cranky bitch, but she had this thing for cherry coke. Apparently Hell didn't have carbonated beverages. She would answer all of my questions for a few twelve packs. She'd never rat out her people if this was Hell's doing, even if I offered her a lifetime supply.

That was my straightforward plan. The challenging

project was going to be writing a spell to hack the Library of the Profane itself. Dorian and Bram were my main suspects. They'd both been in the basement looking up primordial gods and both of them had been given library cards with all access.

I gave Bram his test, and I knew the results had to be accurate, even if I didn't understand them. That left Dorian's test, which I didn't witness with my own two eyes.

I already knew Silvaria would do anything for Dorian. I'd always questioned his library card, even before I found out he was a shitty lay.

I had two warlocks, a god, and a vampire here with me. I think Balthazar had a crush on Reyson, or perhaps he just liked the way his blood smelled because he took very little convincing to join us. All my spare rooms were getting converted to bedrooms full of hot guys that fate sent to help me.

I needed to call a meeting. The library was closed for the night. I called everyone into the TV room because it had the most places to sit. I had their full attention. I could get used to this.

I considered summoning a demon I work with sometimes and asking her straight if Hell had a reason to raise Reyson but if they had, she wouldn't tell me. She trades information for cherry coke, but if she doesn't want to answer a question, she won't. No matter what I offer.

"Both men who were in here researching primordial gods have ties to demons. Dorian made a deal, and Bram works for one. They were both given all-access, just like all of you. I gave Bram the test myself, but a board member used her key to sneak in here while I was sleeping to administer Dorian's.

"One of these men might be part of this team, and the other might be the one who started all of this. One of the tests has to be wrong. We need to find a way to hack the magic here and see if they altered a test. I don't know how it would be possible, but none of this shit happening right now should be possible."

"I think you've already made up your mind, Ripley," Felix said. "It's an excellent idea, and I'll help. All signs point to Dorian since you didn't give him the test yourself, but I've dealt with demons too. They always have an agenda. They do nothing unless they get something out of it. Even if Bram isn't responsible for any of this, he still wants something, and he was in the basement for a reason. You can't trust anyone from Hell."

Balthazar just yawned.

"That's a little racist. People say that about vampires too."

"And my entire family because of Lucifer, especially after the whole demon thing," Gabriel said.

Surprisingly, he knew that part of his history and I didn't like them talking to Felix like that.

"Let's face it. We know nothing about Hell, except that demons like making deals and tricking people. Demons can be bribed for information. Bram had a very calming aura for a Hellhound. I didn't get bad vibes from him, but that doesn't change the fact he was one of only two people researching primordial gods before that hedge witch showed up with a body. We know every single person who was involved with this made a deal with a demon. We have to look at all options, even if Bram didn't leave a terrible impression on me."

"My grimoire is full of blood magic," Gabriel said. "I can dig into it and see if I can find something."

"I started a new grimoire since mine is gone," Felix said. "I've never tried to fiddle with a magical library before, but back in my day, I was fantastic with magical wards. I can fiddle with it."

Balthazar just clapped his hands.

"My profession is not exactly legal... I can hack anything."

Reyson was not one to be upstaged.

"I could just touch the bowl and answer your question, but I might break the entire library."

"Okay, house rules. We're going to figure this out, but we aren't doing anything until we are certain nothing will get broken in the process. I get you have powers none of us can even comprehend, Reyson, but please don't use them in here if it's going to destroy anything."

Reyson just winked at me.

"I'd never break your library, my witch."

I just had this feeling deep in my gut that as much as he didn't want to, Reyson was eventually going to break my shit.

CHAPTER 22
GABRIEL

What the actual fuck had I gotten myself into? And why did I feel like I'd come home with these people? It was drilled into me from a young age to leave demons the fuck alone. I had never even summoned one for information, which was considered normal among witches and warlocks. It was only frowned upon if you made a blood deal for favors.

I would never give my blood to one of those fuckers after what had gone down with my ancestor, but there were times I almost wished I could summon one to trade information. I never did. My ancestor that made the deal got precisely what they'd asked for, and it was a horrible power that no one person should have. The payment came due, and they didn't want to pay up. They did horrific things in the process of avoiding the demon trying to collect payment.

I didn't know Dorian or Bram, but I didn't trust either of them. Why was Dorian Gray this famous playboy who got a book written about him and had fangirls on this library board despite the fact everyone knew about his deal? Most everyone else kept that a secret because it would mean an instant shunning. I didn't trust Bram because he came from Hell. The demon who made a deal with my ancestor should have told him no when he heard what he was asking for. Some things shouldn't be gifted.

I should have been noping right out of this library because it reeked of demons. So... why wasn't I?

I guess because even if it wouldn't change the entire world's opinion of my family, none of these people cared about the whole demon thing, or that we were descendants of Lucifer. They never brought it up once, even if they all had opinions on deals with demons. It was like they understood what the entire world couldn't. My ancestor made that deal. I didn't.

And I liked these people. Ripley was sweet to me as long as I didn't break any rules in her library. I had no idea how her familiar could change like that, but he was very grumpy and snarky. Felix was brutally honest, and I respected that.

I couldn't believe I was in the company of a fucking god, and Reyson was a little weird. He'd pretty much decided as soon as he laid eyes on her that Ripley was going to be his wife. Who did that, anyway? She must have the patience of a saint because she allowed him to stay here, even with the whole wife thing and all the weird shit he said. He also seemed to have a steady diet comprised exclusively of Frappuccinos and weird flavored Oreos.

Balthazar was the newest addition, and he just seemed like a horny fuck. He was continually staring at both Ripley and Reyson like he wanted to eat them or fuck them, or do both at the same time. Ripley just ignored it, but Reyson was eating up every minute of it.

Researching how to hack a magical library without breaking it was going to take a lot of work. I wasn't afraid of it. This is what I was meant to be doing. I always knew I could do great things with my magic if given a chance. No one ever wanted to give me one though, at least not until I set foot in this library.

It meant a lot to me. I was putting all the education they allowed me to have to good use. I didn't want this to end if we won. I wanted to stay here, in this library, with all these strange people that accepted me.

I was officially off tarot research. We'd figured out just a smidge of it but recognized that if someone had cheated their way into the library then that needed to be our top priority. I just couldn't figure it out.

A board member could have totally cheated the system to get Dorian in, and I was pretty sure anything out of Hell could have figured it out too. Reyson put some magic into the air to draw anyone involved in this to the library.

We needed to figure this out before Hell felt the call.

CHAPTER 23
FELIX

This was bollocks. I was with Ripley for the entire application process. I was watching her back in the warehouse when applicants were killing each other. Fuck, some of those people were trying to kill familiars to get to their witch or warlock. I was there for her entire training on the magical system and different sections. The training was rigorous, and we both could have died in that warehouse.

They drilled it into her to trust the system. It was supposed to be flawless and unable to be cheated. Yet, someone had, and they hadn't taught us a single thing about what to do when that happened. She could have called the board and asked, but seeing as the board was potentially compromised, that may not have gotten us very far.

Silvaria would have been instrumental in getting the painting stored here. Still, if she gamed the system to get Dorian in here, Ripley would have been blamed for it, even if Silvaria was the one that cheated and used her key to sneak in when she knew Ripley was sleeping.

I had to protect Ripley, which meant trying to figure out how to magically hack a library.

We were all sitting at Ripley's desk in the library. No one else touched by Reyson's magic had appeared just yet, so we didn't even get the chance to use the truth potion. The library had been pretty quiet, to be honest.

People came here when they needed information, or fresh werewolf porn. They came when they had a need for information or smut.

A few people came in for information and the system was working like it was supposed to. Ripley sent them off. Thankfully no one needed her to do any magic. As the librarian, she assisted with spells and necromancy, and she read tarot cards for anyone who asked. People were only here for the books today though, so we were all hard at work.

Ripley and Gabriel had their grimoires out. I had a new one I'd just started with spells I remembered. Gabriel had a ton of dark spells in his and a lot of useful information on blood magic. Balthazar had a ton of information on blood that I didn't know because I didn't bite people like a savage and drink it from them. Still, I was grateful he was here contributing.

Reyson was just glaring at the bowl like he could figure it out without breaking it. Honestly, I wished he could because our magical library training didn't cover this, and I didn't have a clue where to start.

"Blood is blood," Balthazar said. "You can't change the properties of it, but you can pollute it with drugs and a shitty diet. Those people don't taste good, and I avoid eating them. That wouldn't trick this place. There used to be a time when vampires were serious apex predators. When we fed, we did it to the death. Supernaturals are good eating because you get the extra hit of magic. People would do all sorts of shit to make their blood less appealing, including magic. It didn't save them in the end, because you can't change the innate magic in your blood."

That was just gross, but we all got the picture. It didn't help us because it still didn't answer how someone got past the blood magic here.

"We've got a god here. I think we should use him," Balthazar said, looking dreamily at Reyson.

"That would be ideal, but we'd all get kicked out if the library breaks," Gabriel said.

"Let's avoid breaking my library, k?" Ripley said.

These blokes right here. They were going to have to realize this was Ripley's profession, and she took pride in it. Plus, this library had been around since the Salem Witch Trials. We should respect it.

"Can I break someone if they show up because of my magic?" Reyson asked. "I know you have the truth potion, but I can sense connections. If I can find one person involved, then I can probably trace it to the source from them."

"I get y'all are the friendly type of witches and warlocks, but come on. We've got Chaos. Why not let him have a little fun? He's probably bored senseless being cooped up here," Balthazar said.

Based on the way that wanker was eye fucking Reyson and Ripley, it was pretty obvious what kind of fun Balthazar had in mind. Based on how obsessed Reyson was with the werewolf porn, he would be totally down with it. Except Reyson wasn't exactly Captain Obvious. He only had eyes for Ripley. Except when he was asking her for a wolf to sample. This was a pretty shitty team if you ask me. No one needed to be thinking about sex or shifter cock with everything else going on. Reyson could have contributed way more and well before now, but he was so preoccupied with finding a new name, even though he'd had countless names since time began.

Yeah, I got we were supposed to do this together, but I had more at stake. Ripley was my witch. I'd known her the longest and knew her the best.

She wasn't some obsession of mine that I randomly decided I was going to marry at first sight. I wasn't here because I like the way her blood smelled.

The only person here whose motivations I could understand was Gabriel. I'd protect Ripley until I couldn't anymore. I got the feeling Gabriel would, too, since she was probably the first witch that didn't hold his family name against him. People seemed to have forgotten basic decency since I last had a body.

"I'm fine where I am," Reyson said. "I've got my books and my witch. I can hold off exploring this unknown world until my witch is safe."

Yeah, Captain Obvious. The fun Balthazar was talking about could have been had in any of the bedrooms in Ripley's apartment. Balthazar just rolled his eyes and settled his shit down. He was going to have to try much harder than that. I needed to get them to focus.

"I agree, we needed to be making the most of Reyson's abilities as much as possible, but it would be best if no one knows he's back until we're ready for them. The scene needs to be set. The supernatural community is diverse, but gods haven't walked among us for a long time. Some people will view it as a good thing and line up to kiss Reyson's arse. Others will view him as a threat and kill Ripley for bringing him back."

"Not with me here. They could all band together and trick me into a tomb again, but the only reason I hadn't come back for so long until Ripley forced me was that I chose not to."

Gabriel just grunted.

"I think we can all agree Ripley needs to be protected, but we're a team. We need to look out for each other, which means concentrating on figuring this out.

"Ripley thinks someone shouldn't have a library card. If we can figure out who that is, maybe we can reverse what they did and keep them out of here. You ban people from this library, right? What usually happens?"

It was pretty damned funny the first time I saw someone banned from the Library of the Profane. The look on their face was priceless.

"The library is sentient, and it's tied to blood. When people come in, they have to bleed in the bowl unless it's fiction. Those are the only books allowed to leave the library. If something has changed since they approved you, the library knows when it gets the blood. The text I see turns red, and the library forcibly removes you with magic. It also puts a curse on you. From that day forward, even if you want to visit and you've been there before, you'll never be able to find the Library of the Profane again."

The first time that went down, Ripley and I had been told what was going to happen, but seeing it in person was something else. Ripley barely had time to react when the text came up red. She didn't even get the chance to inform the shifter standing there that they had been banned.

A mini tornado kicked up in the middle of the library, plucked the shifter up, and whisked them out the front door. It didn't stop until he was well off the property. It didn't look like a gentle exit either. We saw him trying to stand up in the distance, looking pitifully nauseous. When he finally got to his feet, he began to wretch and ended up vomiting. His hair was everywhere.

He stood outside the property, pulling a right Karen! He couldn't see the library, but he knew he was just there. He kept shrieking for a manager to come out and let him back in.

It was indeed one of the best Karen tantrums I'd seen in a long time, and we didn't get many of those in the library. It was beautiful.

"The more I learn about this place, the more fucked up it gets," Balthazar said.

"I agree with you, Ripley," Gabriel said. "The only reason either of those men didn't get banned when they gave their blood and asked to look at the books on primordial gods is that something has happened to the magic."

"Unless the library let them in because it wanted Reyson back and intends on banning them at their next visit," Balthazar said.

That was a possibility none of us had considered. Maybe the horny vampire had his uses after all. They built the Library of the Profane over the mass graves of witches burned during the Salem Witch Trials, but many people thought the Puritans stopped there. The truth was they burned a lot of other supernaturals, too, and had a dumpsite for the bodies.

It was massive, too, because the Library, the museum, and the academy were all built atop it, and all three were sentient. It took the entire supernatural community to reclaim those lands and tie the spirits to the buildings. This had once been a very haunted place, home to a lot of angry spirits. They couldn't pass on because they weren't given the rites by their community.

The spirits were given a purpose instead. The sheer number of bodies and how decomposed they were made digging up the graves to identify them and give them their last rites practically impossible. I wasn't there, but I knew that they would have at least made an attempt if it had been an option.

A lot of witches and warlocks gathered at the site to communicate with the dead. Shifters were there for their protection, and vampires helped with some of the blood magic.

It finally came to me. We didn't need to figure out how to get around a complicated blood spell and figure out who tricked it without breaking the library.

We needed to just ask the spirits.

CHAPTER 24
RIPLEY

I *loathed* communing with spirits. They had all this knowledge now that they were dead, but I'd rather ask a conniving demon. Demons could be bribed. They wanted something in return for their information—something I could easily buy too, most of the time. I really lucked out finding a demon with a cherry coke fetish because some had far more expensive tastes.

Spirits just didn't want to be dead anymore, or they wanted to move on. It was against the law to bury anyone without giving them the proper rites. If someone found out, you just disappeared one day. There were rumors that those people were tortured until they revealed what they had done with the bodies so those spirits could be put to rest.

Most everyone performed the rites unless you were up to something you weren't supposed to be, and didn't want a body found. Even if you were disposing of a person you'd just killed then the rites could still be performed, but criminals didn't care about that kind of thing.

The only thing spirits ever wanted in return for their information was revenge or help finding their bodies so they could move on. I knew *how* to commune with the dead, but after doing it a few times, I preferred to summon demons if I couldn't find the information anywhere else.

Though I had little choice this time. Felix was right.

The Library of the Profane's magic was stitched together with blood magic, witchcraft, and spirits. Trying to get around all the blood magic and spells without breaking the entire library was going to be impossible. The spirits would know.

I picked the one windowless room in my apartment for the magic that required total darkness and concentration. Gabriel, Felix, and Reyson were here to help. Balthazar was going a little stir crazy. Reyson was utterly oblivious to all his attempts at getting a bedroom romp with a god. Balthazar wanted a little more action, and I didn't need his commentary during this. If someone offended the spirits, they wouldn't talk to us.

Balthazar was off hunting down the hedge witches that were in here with Hettie. He was literally on my laptop for no more than two minutes before he had their names and addresses. He even found out the top-secret location of where their coven met. No self-respecting witch put that online for people to find. I doubted the hedge witches did either, but Balthazar still found something. I was starting to understand why he was on our team.

I didn't even have to tell him not to hurt them. He

said he would watch from a distance to see if he could gather any actionable intel. Granted, I hardly knew the vampire, but I felt okay sending him out to spy. I had a suspicion that he was planning some sort of epic threesome with Reyson and me, but I trusted him to spy on some hedge witches.

Balthazar was already gone and I had everything set up to contact the spirits. I had protective runes drawn in chalk on the floor and every single black candle I owned lit. I had two warlocks and a god sitting in the protective circle with me to channel. I would need all three of them because Lilith knew how many spirits would answer my call, given the sheer number of people that'd been murdered on these grounds.

We all linked hands. Gabriel and Felix knew the right words. Reyson didn't.

"You need to chant *Imperiteus Strixundis* with us, Reyson."

Fucking god. He just chuckled and shook his head like none of us had summoned the dead before.

"Show yourselves, spirits!" Reyson yelled.

Only a fucking god would be so rude to ghosts. This entire process was to call them, so they were actually in a decent mood when they answered. After the chanting, you had to invoke Lilith's name and do a lot of asskissing to get them to show themselves. You just *did not* bluntly order a spirit to appear like that.

Every single flame on the black candles in the room jumped to ten feet high. A ghastly wind kicked up. Great. The spirits were pissed, and there were a lot of them in here.

"Calm yourselves!" Reyson boomed.

I'd never heard his voice like that before, it was

usually so silky-smooth and a little playful, but now it roared and echoed off the walls. The wind died down and the flames diminished. A single solitary spirit was in the room with us. She was dressed in Puritan garb and dripping wet. She must have been drowned instead of burned. Fucking humans and those witch tests they designed. *Everyone* drowned if you held them underwater, witch or not.

"Speak your peace, god," she spat. "What do you want?"

That was certainly new.

Even if you prepped them right and did this the witch way, they never got right to the point. She didn't even demand something for these answers. It was good having a god on your side.

"Someone was given a library card that wasn't supposed to be. I have questions about that."

"Yes, they were. A promise was made, and we accepted."

"Speak, witch! What was promised, and who was the exception made for?"

The spirit started laughing, and it wasn't enjoyable to watch or hear. It was a sickening cackle, like she was laughing and choking on water at the same time.

"Some of us are content with our new purpose in the buildings erected on this land, but some of us have grown discontented. We long to be released. We care not what you are or what power you possess. We want only what they promised to us."

Reyson just flicked his wrist.

"Away with you, witch."

It was like a black hole opened in my spell room and sucked her through. We got a little, but not all, of the information. Spirits didn't like to cooperate on a good day, but especially not when a promise had been made. Reyson wasn't done yet.

"One of the good spirits of this library better get their ass in here and explain."

Gabriel and Felix had their mouths wide open, like they were catching flies, and I was just sitting there trying not to laugh.

EVERY ONE OF my classes at the Academy of the Profane on dealing with spirits had stressed the importance of placating them and being careful what you promised them. They took it personally if you reneged and could make your life miserable in retaliation. My professors also drilled into us that they seldom did anything without some sort of vow being made, unless you stroked their egos.

Reyson was just up here in my circle bossing spirits around, and he hadn't promised them a fucking thing. After dealing with a few shades myself, it was fucking beautiful to watch.

A child appeared before us. Tendrils of smoke were wafting up from the transparent spirit. That just made me fucking angry. The Puritans had killed a fucking *child* when someone slipped up and let the supernatural be known to them. Reyson visibly softened and got a little nicer when he saw we were dealing with an eight-year-old.

"I'm so sorry," Reyson said. "You didn't deserve what happened to you. What is your name?"

"My name is Saul. Most of us have come to terms with our fate. We enjoy protecting these buildings because it helps keep our existence a secret. What happened to us then has a better chance of never being repeated. Still, there are those of us who have never been happy being tied to these buildings and think something could have been done to give mass rites to everyone in the graves, but that was not possible. The rituals are different for every supernatural group, and there were just so many of us who died.

"You aren't the first to try to talk to us. Every time someone summons us, someone who is not happy with our lot asks for the knowledge to perform a mass rite and release us.

"Almost everyone says that information doesn't exist, and it would involve destroying all of these historic buildings to exhume us.

"Until recently. Someone claimed to have the knowledge and the power to get every single building built on our graves torn down. Most of us thought she was lying but she revealed herself to be demon tainted. A lot of us here want to leave things as is, because we don't trust someone who has made a deal with a demon to release us, and it not be part of her payment later on. Others are so unhappy that they are willing to risk it. All she wanted in return was for someone who wasn't supposed to be allowed in to have a library card."

I would not let Reyson run this show. This was my library, and I had questions.

"Who promised those mass rites, and who did they let in?"

"Someone who was abusing their power and shouldn't be anywhere near this place. She's responsible for helping run this library. She wanted to allow another demon tainted individual access to information here. We wanted no part of it, but enough of us did that they could grant her request and keep the library from banning him every time he visited."

"Do you have names?" I asked.

"We don't deal in names here. We barely remember our own. The witch and the man she let in were both very vain and paid too much attention to their appearances. Both the man and the woman heavily painted their faces."

I didn't need a name. That was enough for me. I had my suspects. Now I had my proof. Silvaria made a deal with the spirits to sneak Dorian in. So I knew who did it, but not why.

Why had everyone involved in this made a deal with a demon, and how did Bram play into all this?

CHAPTER 25
BALTHAZAR

I didn't ask to get recruited by some team of magical superheroes trying to stop whatever was going on, but I was bored and between jobs. Honestly, the god and the witch were the sexiest things I'd ever laid eyes on. I would love to be in a sandwich between them. One had to set frequent life goals, and that was now a big one.

I joined up, and now I needed to prove myself useful. My job was underground, but it involved finding things that didn't want to be found. Sometimes it was money that had been secreted away in offshore bank accounts that found its way into my account. I found artifacts before they ended up at the Museum of the Profane. I've been known to find wayward people too. I never admitted this to anyone, because I had a reputation to uphold, but the supernatural police had brought me in a few times.

Hunting down a few hedge witches was child's play. I could watch without them ever knowing. Witches never advertised their coven's meeting place, and it was no different this time. Except if you had the name of a few coven members, you could hack the GPS on their phones and quickly figure that out.

It was usually a remote piece of real estate the coven had banded together to purchase and then passed down through the ages. This was no different. The hedge witches met in a greenhouse near the forest, and I could easily hear and see inside.

"What do you think happened to Hettie? She should have been back with him by now."

"I think Hettie is long dead. I told you we shouldn't have gotten involved in this."

"*I* think Hettie is still at the library. The librarian wasn't very nice to us. I think she figured out something was up before she raised the god and is torturing poor Hettie until she talks."

"We owe it to Hettie to go back there and check."

"You saw what happened the last time we went there. People surrounded the library. We barely blinked, and suddenly, we were in the middle of the highway. I'm not fucking with that again."

"We shouldn't have gotten involved with this. I get Hettie is in love with Dorian, but we are going down a dangerous path. We tried to help him resurrect a god. The god might not have wanted to be brought back here and murdered Hettie."

One witch sighed.

"Well, we're involved now, whether or not we want to be. That librarian saw every single one of our faces. Even if she stopped the resurrection, she's got access to an entire library to figure out who we were trying to raise. Once she figures it out, we're in deep shit."

"You're right. Maybe we can give her something to

spare us. Why did Dorian want the god so badly? Did Hettie ever say?"

"Hettie was sweet, and I loved her to death, but she always got stupid around men. She would have helped him, even without knowing."

"Yes, but *we* aren't stupid. We should have asked questions instead of going all sisterhood of witches and helping her. We're in deep shit here."

"We'll figure it out. We always do."

They knew nothing, so I was free to use my vampire speed to get to where I'd stashed my bike. I had done some fucked up shit for love in the past, but I can't say I'd ever convinced an entire coven to raise a god for some dick. Ripley was pretty vocal about it being some nasty dick, too. People should have standards. It might be pretty, but if the sex was terrible and they asked you to do bad things, walk away.

The hedge witch Dorian convinced to do his dirty work died for it, too. Many people were going to die because Dorian Gray was plotting something. I had a feeling Ripley had gotten information from the spirits at the library. She probably confirmed it was Dorian who wasn't supposed to be there.

Sure, I was an asshole to everyone, but even I had my limits. I needed to get back and let everyone know the hedge witches that weren't dead weren't involved in this. They were helping a sister witch and didn't deserve to die for it.

CHAPTER 26
GABRIEL

I was so fucking angry. I stormed out of the room after the spirits left. Five hundred years of being treated like shit by the magical community, all the while most of those people had their own deals with demons. This Silvaria was clearly a respected witch or she wouldn't be on the board of the Library of the Profane. Look what she did with it. It was so fucked up she'd gained that much power, and I couldn't even get a job in the magical community.

I was sitting on one of the Library of the Profane's balconies and just glaring at the grounds. It was beautiful out here. The flowering jasmine grew everywhere and I could spot herbs and flowers meant for spells all over the place. There was a tall rowan tree at the entrance for protection. I could smell the heady scent of the flowers mixing from up here.

It was hard to believe this was a mass grave. The only way anything could have grown on cursed grounds like this was if the spirits were happy. No one had any reason to think any of the shades here hated their lot because nothing was dying.

The balcony door opened, and Ripley joined me. She handed me a cold beer and took the chair next to me. I didn't *really* want to be alone, but I was used to it. I didn't have anyone to talk about this shit with. My family just accepted it and went about their menial human jobs. If I complained, they told me it was just our lot in life, and we couldn't change it.

"That was fucked up," Ripley said, sipping her beer.

I wrenched the cap from mine and took a huge sip.

"What do you intend to do with what you've learned?"

"I've never liked Silvaria. She's one of those uber-wealthy witches who can trace their lines all the way back to Salem and even further back, she has ties to old royalty in Europe. She doesn't see being on the board as a position of honor she needs to take seriously. It's all just bragging rights for her.

"I love this place. My sister is the lead curator at the Museum of the Profane. We both graduated from the Academy. My family didn't come from a famous line, and my parents weren't wealthy. They gave us scholarships to the Academy of the Profane, and we had to fight to get our jobs.

"We weren't the top choices. They would have wanted someone from one of the ancient lines or someone who came from old money. If it had been up to the boards instead of the spirits, Ravyn and I never would have been invited to the academy, and our applications wouldn't have been given a second glance.

"There's so much fucking snobbery in the magical community, and a lot of those hypocrites are up to far worse shit than what they shun people for. I've had some desperate people come in here to get curses broken, and they refuse to name who did it. Draw your own conclusions."

I should have been angry at what she just said. Yeah, she didn't have some ancient lineage or money, but they still gave her more chances to succeed than I was ever given. I wasn't angry with her though, she couldn't help that any more than I could help how people reacted to me.

"Is that why you didn't even react when you found out who I was? Most people do it to my face, but some people try to hide it. It always slips right before they put the mask on. You could have seen the name John Smith based on your reaction."

"Because all of that is just so stupid. Everyone is so hung up on their ancestors, like someone who lived a thousand years ago somehow makes you a better person or a shitty person. What matters is who *you* are and what *you* do. Many people in our community have all this respect they didn't earn because one of their family members did something great way back in the middle ages. It's stupid. We give them a pass for shitty attitudes and shitty things, and they don't deserve it."

I just let out a bitter laugh. I hoped it reached all the way to the moon. Orion sighed and tightened around my neck. He was asleep, but always watching. How did I manage to find this witch? She was damn near perfect.

"Not everyone feels that way."

"This is pretty fucking major, Gabriel. Silvaria made a deal with a demon and the spirits here to sneak someone into the library. She abused her power. There were a ton of people outside my library who were demon tainted. If we can stop this before it goes full apocalypse, it's going to rock the entire magical community."

I sat back and sipped my beer. I agreed with her. People were going to go down when this got out. I didn't want to talk about that. Who was this witch? I finally had her alone without the god lurking around. Orion was curled around my neck. I could tell he had gone to sleep when she showed up to give us some privacy.

I was here because we drew the same tarot spread, but Orion was always hissing in my head to get to know her better, but I kept ignoring him because I thought it was pointless. I would be out of here once this was over. Most people didn't want the burden of my name hanging around them.

I was starting to think Ripley was different. Everyone here was, even the god. I hoped I would have at least made a few friends when this was over. I wanted to know more about this witchy librarian.

"Can we talk about something else?" I asked.

"That's why I came out here. It means something that you're here. I'm not sure what, but I wanted some alone time with you. Felix is keeping Reyson occupied by showing him the *Star Wars* movies. Reyson may be a little high maintenance but is easily distracted with television and werewolf porn!"

I started laughing, and it felt like ages since the last time I'd found anything even remotely funny. It was just so fucked up. Reyson looked every inch the god, and I watched him command those spirits quite easily. Except sometimes the shit that came out of his mouth was just so bizarre. I had to remember all of this was new to him, and he hadn't been on Earth in a very long time.

"Have you tried showing him actual porn videos?"

Ripley started choking on her beer.

"Lilith, no! I don't want to give him any ideas. The dude has already decided I'm going to be his wife. Watching porn together is technically fifth date material. I'll just stick to Doctor Who and movies for now."

"Most women would jump at the chance to marry a god. He's good looking, too."

"He's sex on a stick, but don't tell him I said that. I want more than a seven-foot-tall Adonis with cosmic powers. When I get married it's going to be because I'm in love. I will admit though, that he's growing on me. He's just so precious with his Oreos, Frappuccinos, and reactions to everything related to current events. And he is trying."

"I never thought I'd get married. I didn't think anyone would want to."

"Why? You're totally sex on a stick, too. Someone would totally hit that if you gave them a chance."

I tipped my beer bottle at her.

"People totally do, but they don't want to put a ring on it."

She clinked her beer bottle against mine.

"Don't I know it. I have horrible luck with people in general. It's only fitting the one guy who wants to stick around is Chaos personified."

"Sounds like you just met some shitty men because you're pretty amazing."

She stopped to regard me for a minute. Ripley chewed her bottom lip like she wanted to say something, but wasn't sure she should. She finally shrugged and broke into a huge grin.

"The same with you and women because you're pretty cool. Tell me something about you that no one else knows."

There was just something about this witch. I felt like I could talk to her. She could be pretty snappy when it came to the library, but now that I had her alone, she was just so down to earth.

"This cannot leave this room."

"Do you want to make a blood oath?"

I just laughed. My secrets weren't *that* dark. My family might be descended from Lucifer, and some had that demon problem, and sure I might do some things for the magical community that weren't exactly lily white, but my secrets didn't need a blood oath. I had no problem telling her any of them. I just didn't want it getting around.

"Nothing quite like that. When I was in high school, I had this dream of going to the Academy of the Profane. My family couldn't afford it if I got picked, but I thought I might get a scholarship.

"I was this pasty little nerd who never left their bedroom because I was studying all the time. People weren't just kicking my ass because of my family name. I had this whole geek thing going on.

"When I wasn't studying, I was painting. I learned how to infuse magic into the canvas and pigments. Many people at my high school thought that was a waste. Like simply creating something beautiful with it shouldn't be done, not unless it served a purpose. They were so focused on only using it to hurt people or for personal gain. They did nothing good with it."

"Did you ever get back at them? People tried to do that to my twin sister and me at the Academy since we were scholarship students. We were smart. We played the long game, and our revenge was pretty epic. Exposing those uppity bitches and getting them expelled was beautiful."

"Do I want to know what you did?"

"Nothing illegal. They were using dark magic to cheat their way through school. The Academy of the Profane is not as strict as the library. The spirits choose *most* of the students, but there are several slots reserved for people that can buy their way in. Also, the board there can bump people who were chosen to open a spot for someone willing to pay. You could have very well been chosen for a scholarship, and had your spot taken away for someone with money."

"Fucking witches," I muttered.

That sounded accurate and not totally shocking. I could be bitter about it all day, or I could focus on the future. I was at this library for a reason.

"Did you ever get your revenge, Gabriel?"

"I couldn't then," I said. "Not with my family name. The worst one hired me for a job under the table a few years later. I fucked his wife."

Ripley threw back her head and laughed.

"I love it. Wait a minute! I have a theory about why you're here now! It's the painting thing you just told me about. Dorian Gray is at the heart of this, and we've got his painting in the vault. I don't want to piss any demons off by doing anything to it until we absolutely have to. Maybe you could take a look at it and figure out how to destroy it."

I went to stand.

"Show me this painting."

Ripley grabbed my arm and pulled me back down.

"Later, okay? Reyson is going to be occupied with that movie for a while. It's a pretty night out, and the moon is full. Let's just sit out here and chat."

I could do that. I didn't want to just contribute my magical skills to this. I liked all of these people. Even Reyson and Balthazar were cool.

And I'd never met a witch like Ripley before in my entire life. I wanted to know more.

CHAPTER 27
FELIX

I sincerely hoped I wasn't going to be assigned to god babysitting duties every time Ripley wanted to go off and flirt. Reyson was amusing in that he was like this alien who'd just landed on Earth and was so amazed at the most random shit. Still, he was a god and he acted like it most of the time.

Ripley came back late after hanging out with Gabriel. We'd watched all three *Star Wars* movies. I have never seen someone eat that much junk food in my entire life. Still, he came in handy and he was nice enough to me. He offered to get me food from back home again. I had a hot pork pie in my hand with just a flick of his wrist. Don't ask me how he was doing it, but I wasn't about to complain!

Reyson seemed to have no problem with me sleeping in Ripley's room. I disappeared with her. I had no idea why she wanted me in there with extra bedrooms available. I changed back into the cat and slept on her pillow like I always did. Ripley and I had always been close, but I knew she wasn't afraid of the dark and didn't need me that close. Especially not with Reyson right next door.

It was strange that she was still changing in front of me as if I was still a simple house cat. It wasn't like I could help my reaction. Ripley was an attractive witch, and we were close. I always changed back into the cat as soon as we retired for the night because Ripley was one of those women who ripped her bra off as soon as she got home.

She also slept in tiny, black lace pajamas. I didn't even think about it as the cat, but now that I had a body again, it just seemed inappropriate to sleep in her bed. I nestled myself into her pillow and waited for her to hit the light.

"Felix? Can you change back?"

I *did not* like where my mind was going with this. I'd be totally nude in her bed with her in that teeny lace number if I did that. Still, I'd die for Ripley. I lucked out, getting assigned as her familiar. True, she was snarky, with an awful temper, and she had horrible taste in men, but she had this fantastic heart underneath the hard exterior.

I shifted back and dove under her blanket.

"What's wrong, Ripley?"

"Why do you sleep as the cat when you have your body back?"

"...Because you asked me to stay here, and it's easier that way."

Ripley always just took what she wanted. She pounced on me in an instant, and the next thing I knew, she was snuggled into me. Ugh. I did *not* want to spring an erection through this thin blanket, but my sense of smell was heightened like a shifter now, and Ripley smelled *terrific.*

"What if I don't want things to be easy? You know me better than anyone on the planet, except Ravyn."

"This is dangerous, Ripley. I was your familiar, and Reyson will not take kindly to this. He could take my body away because he thinks you're going to be his wife."

Curse Lilith, I wanted this so badly, and it was so wrong. My cock was so hard, it hurt. It wasn't like I could hide it anymore. The blanket was making a tent in my lap. If only this could have happened without Reyson in the picture. I got the feeling he was a jealous god. He might be okay with us joining this team, but not in her bed like this.

Ripley climbed right on top of me. Fuck! I knew she was aggressive when it came to men, but I'd never been the target before. She ground herself against my cock, and all thoughts of jealous gods flew out of my head.

Until Reyson *kicked the fucking door down.*

Oh, shit. Ripley was not jumping off me either. She just looked at him calmly.

"The cat has been in here for days. This is the first time I've smelled fornication. I was wondering if I put his body together correctly."

What.the.fuck?!

"What is it you want, Reyson? You can't just barge in on me because you smelled sex!"

Reyson was bare-chested and wearing loose

trousers. His hair was loose and spilling over his shoulders. He looked arrogant as fuck, like he hadn't just barged in on the woman he wanted to marry with another man, and he wasn't trying to kill me. He actually looked excited, and the front of his pajama pants was tented out. What the actual fuck was happening? Ripley was still right on top of my cock. I didn't say a damn thing because I didn't want to set him off, and this was painful.

Reyson just bowed his head.

"I would like to watch you and the cat. Please?"

I will say this again. *What.the.fuck?* Chaos just asked my witch permission to watch us have sex. I was still processing the feeling of Ripley on my cock, and now I had a bloody god demanding to watch; and saying please, like he had manners! All I could do was moan when Ripley resumed grinding against me.

"I've never been watched before. It sounds kinky. Only if Felix is okay with it."

At this point, every single drop of blood in my body was firmly in my cock, and I wasn't exactly thinking straight. I would have agreed to have sex in the erotica section of the library, with a packed audience with Ripley doing that to my cock. I could admit having Reyson watch was a bit of a turn on.

"I'm down," I growled, grabbed her hips.

Reyson settled down in an overstuffed chair and started rubbing his cock.

"I gifted the cat his body because I knew the two of you were close, and you weren't comfortable with me yet. I'm a little shocked it took you this long to enjoy it."

"You're okay with this?" Ripley demanded.

I'd like to know that, too, because this was so fucked up. I didn't take Reyson for the type to be okay with sharing *at all*.

"Of course. He is part of our possibilities, just like the others are. The vampire would like to get us both in bed, but I don't think you are ready for that yet."

Well, fuck me. Reyson wasn't as clueless to Balthazar's overtures as we all thought. He was just choosing to ignore them because of Ripley.

Ripley was done talking. She didn't even question what he'd just said about the others. She surged forward and claimed my mouth. She tasted like strawberries, and the girl knew how to kiss. Still, I didn't particularly appreciate having sex flat on my back like a dead fish. I grabbed her waist and flipped her on her back.

I buried my face in her neck and bit her ear. Ripley let out a little hiss and yanked my hair. Yes! A bit more hair pulling, please. I looked down at her and smirked.

"You have way too many clothes on."

Her clothes barely covered anything, but they were still too much. I yearned to feel her naked flesh pressed up against mine. I snapped my fingers, and all her clothes disappeared. I'd seen Ripley nude countless times before, but I'd never really stared at her and appreciated it. I started with my fingers at her neck and trailed them down her belly.

Her skin was smooth and velvety soft. Praise Lilith! She was just so beautiful. She wrapped her hand around my cock and tugged at it. This was my first-time having sex since getting my body back, and I hoped I didn't blow it.

Ripley craned her head up and looked at Reyson.

"Did you do that to his cock?"

My head snapped over to the god. What had he done to my cock? I had a perfectly magnificent cock when I was a warlock. I jumped back to inspect it.

"I upgraded it. The fiction inspired me in the library."

Why did he have to mess with my cock? There were soft ridges all down the shaft now, that weren't there before now that I was erect.

"Put my knob back this instant!" I demanded.

"You can shift into a cat. I made your cock similar to a cat's. It'll feel better for Ripley. Trust me on this."

Ripley wrapped her hand around my cock again.

"I wouldn't mind trying it, but if it bothers Felix, you should put it back."

Ripley might not want to admit it, and she would need time, but Reyson could see the possibilities. Ripley would eventually be with Reyson and, if he was correct, the others, too. I didn't know where I'd fit in her life then, but I needed to stand out. I could keep the ridges on my cock, for now, to see if she liked it. It would give me an edge over the others at least.

If her eyes didn't roll back in her head, Reyson was so fixing my fucking cock.

I shoved Ripley back onto the bed. I worshipped her body with kisses. I nipped and sucked her perfect breasts until she was writhing beneath me and pulling my hair. I kissed every inch of her until I got to where I wanted to be. I settled myself between her thighs and gave her clit a long lick.

Fuck. She tasted divine. I intended to eat her up. I lapped at her clit to the sounds of her cries and

Reyson's moans. Maybe I was a little perv, but it was a massive turn on having him sitting there watching. She was slick, and I easily slid two fingers inside her. I finger fucked her as I devoured her clit before turning my fingers up to massage that special spot inside her.

I felt her cum on my tongue. Her entire body tensed and she let out a massive cry as her orgasm overtook her. I was so fucking turned on at the moment, it wasn't funny. I licked every last inch of her orgasm out of her and crawled up to pull her to my chest.

Ripley's hand found my cock again.

"I want this," she said breathlessly.

I pressed her onto her back and nipped at her neck.

"Are you up to date on your birth control spells?" I asked.

"Of course. They don't just keep me pregnancy and disease-free. It stops that nasty zit on my chin from popping out."

"Even that is sexy right now," I groaned.

I guided myself into her, and it was just unreal. She was so bloody tight and wet. I looked down into her expressive eyes, and she bit her lip seductively. My hips started moving, thrusting in and out of her. Ripley moaned and raked her nails down my arm.

"Scratch me and pull my hair," I growled.

She gave me exactly what I wanted. I sped my hips up, and Ripley's cries were music to my ears.

"I know you don't like it, but your new cock is magic!" she cried as she clamped down on it.

Fuuuuck. This was nothing short of amazing. I managed to last way longer than I thought I would, considering I hadn't had sex in a very long time. I kept a punishing pace until I felt that familiar tingle in my spine. I waited until I felt Ripley cum again, then let go. I threw back my head and roared as I came.

I collapsed and pulled her into my chest. *And I started purring.*

Fucking god!

CHAPTER 28
RIPLEY

Oh, my Lilith! I was in a mood after my romp with Felix. Reyson was getting up to go back to his room. Don't ask me why I did it, but I invited him in bed to just sleep. I slept sandwiched between Reyson and Felix, who had started purring. It was fucking adorable, and I'd never slept that well in my entire life. Reyson certainly knew how to snuggle.

I didn't want to get out of bed, and I didn't really have to. The library wasn't open on the weekends, so it was officially my day off. I yawned and stretched. Felix nuzzled my neck, and Reyson was gone. Where was he? And what was that smell? Something delicious was coming from the kitchen.

I threw a robe on and padded out with Felix. Reyson was in my kitchen with a vast spread laid out on the table. It looked and smelled amazing. He beamed up at me from over the top of an entire side of pig.

"Hello, my witch. I made breakfast."

"You certainly did. It looks awesome."

Gabriel and Balthazar stumbled in next.

"Oh, holy shit," Gabriel sighed, looking at the food.

"It's not blood, but even I can say that looks amazing."

"Do you need to eat?" I asked.

Vampires could eat human food, but they needed blood pretty often. Balthazar flashed his fangs at me.

"I nipped a bite when I was spying on the hedge witches. But, if you're offering…"

We could talk about that later. We needed to talk about what we learned. I knew why Gabriel was with us now. I was seeing why Balthazar was too if he could locate the hedge witches like that.

"Were they where they were supposed to be?"

He just gave me a toothy grin.

"They always are. The hedge witches weren't responsible. They were helping a sister witch because she was into the D she was getting. It was Dorian Gray."

I let out a little growl. Fucking Dorian. Now I felt terrible for smashing cockroach Hettie… almost, that is. She totally would have brought Reyson straight to Dorian like he wasn't an actual person without opinions, and she would have led him directly here if we had let her walk out. As it were, I still didn't know when Dorian and Silvaria were going to come back looking for Reyson.

"We figured that much out. One of the board members made a deal with the spirits here to sneak him in. Oh, my Lilith, Reyson! This is the best food I've ever eaten."

The pig was tender, with just the right amount of fat, and the eggs were so fluffy. I didn't take Reyson for someone so wonderful at cooking. I always just thought he had people to do that for him. He might have acquired the ingredients by magic, but I could see the dirty dishes. He cooked this himself.

"I have my uses, and you worked up quite an appetite last night."

Right when I was coming over to his side, he announced to everyone that I'd had sex last night. Gabriel was focused on his food. Balthazar looked like he hoped Reyson would say more, and Felix seemed quite proud of himself.

I wasn't ashamed of myself. It was hot as shit. When Reyson burst through my door, I thought I would have a god tantrum on my hands, and Felix would insist on his own bedroom after that. When I realized he was sporting an impressive boner and wanted to watch, I was all for it, as long as Felix was.

When I said it was impressive, it was. Almost enough to make it worth going there knowing he had all these ideas about marrying me. *Almost.* I had a big thing about not fucking with people's heads though. I might think it silly Reyson thought we were going to get married, but it was something he really believed, and he was trying his hardest to get me to feel it, too.

I sighed. I *did* lead him on. I had invited him into my bed to sleep with us, *and I liked it.* For being God of Chaos, he snuggled like a total beast. Note to self, no more snuggling with Reyson, even if I liked it. I wouldn't be that woman.

I needed to push that out of my head. I didn't need to be thinking about that at all. It was becoming clear why everyone was here with me, and I needed to make use of their skills. Balthazar would probably get up to some shady shit if he could find a coven location. It was perhaps shady shit for a good cause, or the library would have kicked him out.

I still trusted the system. Yeah, a few spirits helped Silvaria sneak Dorian in because she made them a promise, but they had no reason to help me. I was actively working against her now that I knew the truth. *Something* was trying to help me. Whether it was the good spirits of the library, fate, or some other cosmic force now that Reyson was involved with, I didn't know, but I would use all my resources.

Silvaria was going down. She was my big lead to find out what was going on. I didn't know if Dorian or Silvaria was the ringleader in all of this, and I didn't care. I was coming for both of them and I needed Balthazar for that.

"Balthazar, I'm thinking you've got some skills that aren't exactly... legal."

He just winked at me.

"I'm kind of like the vampire Robin Hood. I only break the law in good ways."

"Could you get into the board members' computers? You could start with Silvaria and go from there."

Balthazar cracked his knuckles and grinned.

"Corrupt witches are so much fun. Did you know some of them have digitized the really nasty shit in their grimoires, just in case the actual books fall into the wrong hands? They don't even encrypt the files. I don't have to be a warlock to know some of those spells are evil. I've found some pretty grandiose memoirs in Word documents like they thought one day, someone was going to respect that shit."

"Not all witches are like that," Gabriel pointed out.

"Oh, I'm not saying they have the market. I've found some pretty incriminating shit on every species in the supernatural world's computers and cell phones. They just do things differently. Vampires get up to some awful shit too, but it's usually just because we're horny or hungry."

"Can you do it?" I asked. "Get into Silvaria's laptop and phone?"

"Yeah, but I'll need my own laptop. Yours is nice, but mine's built for things like that."

"Where is it?" Reyson asked.

"Back home. I was only planning on coming for research."

Reyson snapped his fingers, and a laptop appeared on the table. Balthazar fluttered his long lashes at Reyson.

"You're sweet, big guy."

I rolled my eyes, but I tried to hide my smile—what a team we made. Reyson was trying to woo me to be his wife, but Balthazar was trying to get him in bed. I had a feeling Reyson would be totally down with that too, only if I joined him though. I couldn't say that wasn't intriguing, but it was an idea to revisit later if we ever figured this out.

"While you're doing that, it's time for me to help with what you came for. Minerva Krauss taught me at the Academy of the Profane. We've struck up a bit of a friendship here. I might as well put myself to good use and break your curse. Care to tell me more about it?"

Balthazar seemed to have no shame when it came to just about anything, but I watched his cheeks flush then. I had a pretty good idea of how a bitter witch would curse her ex, but I needed to know precisely what was done."

"Man, it's super embarrassing," he said, running his fingers through his hair.

"I know she cursed your cock, Balthazar. It was pretty common when my sister and I were at the Academy, though Ravyn and I never did it. I think poor Minerva Krauss looked at way more cursed college boy cock than she ever wanted to my sophomore year. It's probably why she never married."

"It's definitely why she never thought about it after that year," Felix said. "Do you remember when Carl streaked across the courtyard? He slowed down long enough for me to see it. That was the ugliest knob I've ever seen, and she had to get up close and personal with it to treat those pustules Clara gave him. You don't have sores on your dick, do you?"

Balthazar turned a little green. Was it something else? Most witches went straight for the dick sores because it was painful and a huge warning sign to other women to stay well away.

"No, thank Nosferatu. If it actually works, it hurts so badly, I can barely stand. Luckily, getting it up in the first place is pretty difficult."

Then why was he hitting on Reyson so hard? Vampires were so weird.

"That's actually a combination of two curses. It's—"

Gabriel just started laughing.

"Man, what on earth did you do to end up with two curses on your dick?!"

Balthazar just glared at him.

"Not a damned thing. She showed up at a meeting

with a client and threw a drink in the poor woman's face because she thought I was fucking her. I almost lost the job, but luckily, I can do things few other people can do. I broke up with her after that, and she didn't take it well. She kept calling and showing up at my house, begging me to take her back.

"I thought she finally got the hint when she started leaving me alone, but that's when the problems started."

"Sounds about right," Gabriel said. "My people can be super petty."

"Anyway, I can break the curses. It's two different potions, but I can bind them together with mugwort to make them less volatile and get the job done. It will also involve some chanting and magic, so I'm going to have to get right up on your dick. I can't just give you the potion."

Balthazar broke into this huge grin. I just knew it was partly because I had to touch his cock and not only because I could break the curse.

Fucking vampires.

CHAPTER 29
REYSON

This was utterly fascinating. I always had people around me the last time I occupied this vessel, but I never worked with them as a team like this. I always considered my gifts to be superior and so could have simply touched Balthazar and healed his affliction without breaking a sweat, but my witch needed to do this.

I had been pretending not to notice, but I knew exactly what the vampire wanted once he had a functioning cock again. Ripley was ignoring it, too, but if I looked at all the possibilities between the three of us, Ripley and I would eventually enjoy sharing the vampire.

It was always so hard to remind myself that I was the only one that could see it all, and the gods had changed. Ripley, Felix, and Gabriel worshipped Lilith. She was a nice witch, but I was so much older than she was. They'd be hanging on to every little tidbit I dropped about the future if my name was Lilith. It was a bit mortifying, really.

Everyone was doing their thing. Ripley, Gabriel, and Felix were mixing potions. Balthazar was glued to his laptop and talking to himself. I needed to do my own thing. They had their powers, and I had all of mine.

What to do first? Dorian Gray was a threat, there was no doubt about that. Still, my witch explained things to me. His deal wasn't made in exchange for horrible powers.

He wanted to be young and pretty forever. Pretty stupid agreement, if you ask me.

I could check with him later. Ripley mentioned a Hellhound had also been given all access. Which meant he could possibly be one of us. He hadn't shown up when I sent magic out for anyone involved to come to the library, but he had been reading the same books Dorian had been reading. Silvaria and Dorian hadn't been back either, which meant they were out of the state.

I needed to find this Bram. I'd only ever met a few Hellhounds. Vicious beasts, but they were treated like slaves. They were tied to a demon who was their master. Sometimes, the demon was too lazy to collect their payment themselves, so they would dispatch their Hellhounds.

Don't ask me what they put them through in Hell, but whatever it was hardened them because it seemed like they felt no pain. My family didn't like it, but we couldn't exactly stop people from making deals with demons. People had free will. We didn't step in when payment was due either. They had free will, but they also had to suffer the consequences of their actions.

I didn't want to witness it in my presence, though. I'd gotten into some scuffles with Hellhounds to get them to take that nonsense away from me. I always won, but they put up a hell of a fight.

I needed to find out if this Hellhound was friend or foe, and I wouldn't be able to ascertain that until I laid eyes on him. Ripley said his name was Bram. I could do a lot with a name. Witches could, too. It was why I wanted to make sure no one had mine this time.

I WENT and sat on the windowsill and crossed my legs. I closed my eyes and tuned out everything and everyone in the room. I needed to focus on the cosmos. I felt myself ascending out of my body and saw a swirl of stars and galaxies.

"Show yourself, Bram."

Something was wrong. I should have instantly astral projected to his location. I could have looked him in the face or seen through his eyes. The only way I wouldn't have been able to lock onto his location immediately was if he were back in Hell. My family had never been there before. Most of us never wanted to visit, but I tried once and found I couldn't.

This didn't bode well. This all tied back to demons and Hell. With all my powers even I couldn't go there. My family didn't create Hell like we did the universe Earth existed in, at least as far as I knew. If one of us did, no one would fess up to it. As far as I knew a new god hadn't been born in ages, but there was a time when my family grew quite rapidly. Some of them I hadn't met, even now.

It wouldn't shock me if one of them created demons and Hell. Just like I helped create Earth and humans with my closest siblings.

It didn't help me figure this out. I needed to lay eyes on Bram to find out if he was friend or foe. If he was a friend, then he had answers and I needed to get him to the library. Ripley was right. The spirits gave us hints about the team her tarot cards foretold by giving them all access to the library.

They gave the Hellhound unrestricted access, and he had answers. I could wait. He would eventually leave Hell. He was in the thick of this and he would be back.

I'd be waiting.

CHAPTER 30
RIPLEY

You weren't technically supposed to mix two potions together. Every single one of my potions professors drilled into us that if one potion would not do the job on its own, you had to spend time in your lab figuring out a brand-new potion to get the job done.

Yet Minerva Krauss was a revolutionary when it came to breaking curses. She figured out a way to combine two potions, even if most of the witching community was still old school and refused to use it. They considered it cheating to throw mugwort in your cauldron to get two potions to cooperate with each other. Frankly, I loved her technique, and used it all the time.

Minerva Krauss tested that theory and proved it worked. Testing potions to create a brand new one when there were two known ones that would do the job was a lot of work. The only way to know if your creation worked or not was to test it; which could sometimes be a disaster. People were willing to get pustules or grow an arm out of their forehead because that was just how shit had always been done, instead of trying something new. Idiots.

Gabriel was engrossed and even he wasn't some ass-backward warlock who was sitting there questioning me and trying to tell me what to do.

"You're seriously telling me mugwort of all things will get these two potions to cooperate? Fuck. I seriously wish I had gotten an invitation to the Academy. I'm dying to meet the witch who figured this out."

"You can if you stick around. She's a real hard ass when she's your professor. She's the only professor ever to give me a C on anything. She's sweet to me now that I'm not her student. We bond over the werewolf porn. She should bring her book back soon. We usually sit in the atrium and have a mini book club about it when she comes back to return her books. She was almost too radical for the Academy of the Profane, but since she'd published so many books and was famous, they made an exception."

"I've read some of her books. I'd probably make an ass of myself if I met her."

I just laughed. Professor Krauss had that effect on people.

"No worse than I did when I was her student. Balthazar, how's it coming along over there?"

"Silvaria is a nasty, nasty witch," Balthazar said.

"Can you bring your cock over here so I can undo the curse on it?"

"Yes, but it's going to hurt my feelings if you don't objectify it."

I just rolled my eyes. He already had his cock out before he made it across the room to me. Reyson had been zoned out at the window but appeared to be back with us. And I caught him peeking. Perv. So was I because I wasn't exactly looking Balthazar in the eye as he stalked towards me like a panther with his cock on display.

"This won't hurt, will it?"

"I don't know. I don't have a cock."

"What about you warlocks? You do. Is this painful?"

Gabriel was just sitting there like all of this amused him. I'd never seen him look this light hearted before. He usually smiled a lot when we were chatting, but never like this. I guess it took a cock curse to really bring out the smiles.

"A witch has never felt the need to curse mine."

"It tingles a bit, but mine has never been doubly cursed," Felix said.

I turned away from Balthazar's cock and stared at Felix.

"You never told me about that."

"It didn't seem prudent when I was stuck as a cat. Some twins were both interested in me. What can I say? I'm a man with fetishes and fantasies. I asked for a threesome, and they cursed me."

"You had that one coming," I pointed out. "I'm a twin."

"Yeah, I totally did. In my defense, I was eighteen and stupid."

"Yeah, well, I was thirty-five and not stupid. I had every reason to break up with her. Can we hurry up and uncurse my dick now?!"

Here goes nothing. I tried to hold his cock so I could get the potion on it, but he sprung a boner and ended up on the floor writhing in pain. I could see bloody tears forming in his eyes, it was hurting him that much. Every single male in the room was feeling sympathy pain watching him.

"I'm going to throw up," Gabriel said.

"Holy shit," Felix said.

"Fucking witches," Reyson growled.

I pounced on Balthazar and tried to pry his hands away from his cock. He was a vampire and had greatly enhanced strength and speed that I didn't have as a witch. My eyes went to Reyson.

"A little help here?"

I had a feeling Reyson could have broken this curse with a simple touch. I don't know why he hadn't offered. Reyson was on the floor in seconds. He laid his palm on Balthazar's forehead and his entire body went limp.

"Thank you," he groaned. "It doesn't hurt anymore. Do it, Ripley."

Oddly, he was still erect during all of this. I wrapped my hands around his shaft and coated his cock with the potion.

"Rectactus Persoulus," I whispered.

The potion sizzled, smoked, then burned off. I thought it was done. That was totally normal. Balthazar's back bowed, and he wailed in pain. He passed out and collapsed on the floor. When I looked down, he was still erect, but his cock was now covered in pustules.

What.the.fuck?

That should have worked, unless the witch that

cursed him was tricky and wove something into her spell to make things worse for him if someone tried to break the curse. I'd be willing to bet that was what she had done. Breaking that kind of magic was tricky.

I'd just made things worse for Balthazar, and I felt horrible about it.

CHAPTER 31
BALTHAZAR

I came to in my bed with a distraught witch and an ice pack on my dick. It looked like I finally had Ripley alone. Man did my dick ever hurt. I groaned and sat up. I peeked under the ice pack, and my fucking cock was covered in oozing sores.

"A little something went wrong with the potion?" I asked.

"I'm so sorry!" Ripley said, flying to the side of my bed. "That witch must have been pissed. She wove a protection into her curse that made it worse when I tried to remove it. I just need to figure out what she did to get it off. Reyson made your erection go down. It may have been stuck that way."

I just chuckled and pulled myself up into a sitting position. I tucked one of her black curls behind her ear.

"I want him to make my cock go up, not down! He's a little clueless."

She smiled at me, and I swear her entire face just lit up when she did that. Note to self—make her smile more. I felt all warm and gooey when she smiled at me.

"Oh, he's aware. He's sure it's going to happen too. He can kind of see the future. I think he wants me to do this so we can get to know each other better. He's playing Cupid."

I felt my eyebrow raise up to my forehead. I had my kinky god fantasies and I flirted, but I didn't think it was possible anything would actually happen. I wasn't flirting with Ripley at all, no matter how much I wanted to, because Reyson had all but licked her to claim her. He could be a little more obvious if he wanted us to hook up.

"How do you feel about that? How do you feel about all of this?"

That was my first question. Ripley had so much shit tossed in her lap. How was she doing? I'd be losing my shit in her situation. She bit her lip and stared at me. God, she looked so adorable when she did that.

"*You're* asking *me how I am* when I just made your cock curse even worse?!"

Was that what was bothering her? Reyson took away the raging erection I got when she touched me. I didn't know if it would hurt if she went for my dick again, and I popped one, but I was fine for now. I just winked at her.

"Did you take a peek when you were touching it?"

She started laughing. It was such a lovely sound. I needed to make her laugh more.

"It was quite impressive. How *are* you anyway?"

I just shrugged. Why was she worried about me with everything else going on? I was much more worried about her.

"Me and my cock are just fine. I'll answer you if you answer me. I'm just fine. How are you?"

"This is all just so weird. I think everyone is giving us time alone for different reasons. Reyson wants us in bed, Felix is doing what Reyson wants, and Gabriel is hoping I cure you."

"So, if the god can see the future, does he see us together?"

Interesting. He said nothing to me. Nor to her, apparently.

"He's never quite so obvious when he talks about what he sees. He sees possibilities, since things change based on decisions. The only thing he's quite clear on is that we will eventually get married," she said, rolling her eyes.

I shrugged. Maybe she didn't see it like I did.

"I've been hitting on him, but I didn't really think anything would come of it. I can see he's into you. He's trying hard, Ripley. That breakfast he slaved over this morning was all to impress you. Everything he does is to impress you, including sticking around to fix this. He could be off in paradise sipping mojitos with the other gods."

"Yeah, I guess; but he hardly knows me."

"Because you won't let him. He's trying, darlin'. I think we all are."

She smiled and touched my cheek. I saw a realization dawn in her eyes. We *all* wanted to get to know her better. I couldn't speak for the others, but this place felt like home to me and these people felt like my family.

"Will you teach me to do my eyeliner like you do yours?"

I let out a squeal worthy of a teenage girl. I *adored* talking makeup, but no one ever wanted to discuss it with me. I'd been wearing eyeliner since high school.

Some fucking shifters tried to beat me up to make some rando man point and learned the hard way not to fuck with vampires. I'd never had a girl ask me for tips before.

I ignored the pain in my cock as I jumped out of bed and ran towards my makeup case. I was *very* particular about my eyeliner and only wore the best brands. I pulled out one of my spare unopened gel pencils and handed it to her.

"A gift. The brand is super important. This is made by Japanese vampires out of unicorn farts and glitter."

"What?"

"Not really, but it's the best eyeliner on the planet. Their proprietary blend is super-secret. Let me watch how you put yours on, and we'll go from there."

I handed her one of my mirrors and set her loose. This was perfect. I had wanted some time alone with both her and Reyson, and now I was finally getting it. She was cool. I knew it upset her about my cock, but I wasn't upset with her.

It just meant we were one step closer to lifting the curse.

CHAPTER 32
RIPLEY

Well, I now knew how to do a banging smokey eye thanks to Balthazar. He had more skills with an eyeliner pencil than I did with a pen and paper. We just sat there, trading makeup tips like nothing more important was going on. He was cool and funny but knew when to get to work.

I still didn't have the cure to his curse. I would have to dig into protection spells in curses to see what they did, and yeah, I was probably going to need Professor Krauss' help. He acted like nothing was wrong, but I could tell he was in a lot of pain. He hid it well.

After we had a few hours chatting, I could see a pinched expression behind his eyes. I realized what it was, and I knew what could make it better. He was a vampire, and he was in pain. I moved my body closer to his and offered him my neck.

"You need to feed, Balthazar."

His nostrils flared, but he didn't move towards me.

"I was going to nip out and find someone to bite."

"Why? I don't mind."

"Your blood smells just as good as Reyson's," he growled.

Balthazar was just so beautiful. He looked so mischievous with his bright red hair and green eyes.

He was long and lean, the way rock stars were built. I wanted him to bite me. I pressed myself closer to him.

"I can be your source."

He groaned and wrapped his arm around my waist. His nose went to my neck, and he traced his nose from my shoulder to my ear. Now, I was the one moaning.

"Are you sure?"

I broke out in goosebumps and got wet as fuck. I'd never been surer about anything in my life. I wanted Balthazar to bite me. I tangled my hand in his red hair and gave it a pull.

"Do it."

He didn't bite me right away. He started nipping and licking my neck. I'd been bitten by vampires before during sex, but it was generally right when they came. I'd never offered to be a source before, but Balthazar was one of us, and he needed to feed. He was a lot gentler than the other vampires I'd been with. At the rate he was going, I would fling him on his back and mount him right there.

I felt his fangs sink into my neck, and I came right there. That had *never* happened to me with another vampire before. Their bites hurt, and the sex was generally bad. I avoided them after the first two. Holy shit. What was Balthazar doing to me? He had me crushed to his chest as my body shuddered.

I was reduced to a quivering mess in his arms. He

pulled away and looked me deep in the eyes as my blood dribbled down his chin.

"Oh, my Lilith! What did you just do?" I moaned. "That's never happened to me with a vampire before."

He just grinned.

"You've been with some selfish vampires then. Our bite can be extremely erotic... if we want it to be. How are you feeling?"

How was I feeling? Fucking amazing. I grabbed him and pulled him down to kiss me. I wasn't quite ready to have sex with him, not yet, but in a way what we had just done was much more intimate. And Balthazar could kiss too.

He pulled away from me, and his eyes were glowing red.

"As much as I want to continue this, I've learned a few things about the witch, Silvaria. We should go back to the others. Your magic tastes wonderful, Ripley."

Right. Silvaria and Dorian. I couldn't turn into a horny trollop until this was all over. Focus, Ripley.

CHAPTER 33
RIPLEY

The guys hasn't been idle while I was off with Balthazar. They were spread out in my living room, and Felix had pulled some of Professor Krauss' curse books from the shelf. He and Gabriel were pouring through them. I expected to find Reyson eating and watching television again, but he wasn't. He was back in the window, zoned out again. What was he doing?

Reyson cracked his eyes open when I came into the room and smiled when he saw me.

"Hello, my witch. I can't find the Hellhound. I think he's in Hell. I've located the witch and the human though, they appear to be having covert meetings with people who have made deals with demons. The witch is in France, and the human is in Hungary. That's why they haven't come back here yet."

"What? Why?!"

"Cuddle pile!" Balthazar yelled, flinging me on the sectional.

I swear, you give a guy a little blood...

He spooned my back and rubbed his face into my hair. I wasn't complaining. I liked this. I just hoped he didn't pop a boner and end up in pain again.

"I can answer that," Balthazar said.

"Silvaria is supposedly traveling for the board, acquiring books for the library. She's been posting on some really dark web forums under an alias in an attempt to find people who have made deals with demons. She's not really saying why. I think all that is being said in person."

"So is Dorian," Reyson said. "I found him with a shifter. He wasn't saying why, but he was trying to coax it from her that she made the deal."

"Why are they trying to find all these people who made deals?" Gabriel said. "Are there a lot of them?"

"More than I suspected. The dark web is the dark web. There's no shame there and everything is anonymous. A lot of people will cop to it, but then won't give any other information. Some people are asking for information on how to make their own deals. Silvaria is promising something better. She's posting that she has access to something that can grant them anything their heart desires without having to sell their soul. I'm guessing she means Reyson."

"Silly witch. I'll eat her alive," Reyson boomed.

Stupid witch was more like it. If she showed up here and tried to boss Reyson around, he was going to get blood all over my library. None of this made sense.

"If they raised Reyson as an alternative to demon deals, why are they trying to market this to people that have already dealt with demons? Most sane people know to stay well away from demons, but wouldn't have a problem asking a god for something because it doesn't involve your soul, or at least, history says it doesn't."

Reyson just shrugged.

"Something else I saw. Dorian thinks Hettie and her coven are babysitting me, but he's getting frustrated he can't reach her by phone. He's feeling the pull to come back here, but he's trying to ignore it. I heard him make a phone call to Silvaria. They seem to think I'm a docile god who is content to be spoiled by hedge witches. They know who I am. They specifically looked for my vessel, but they seem to think a few hedge witches and a little sex can contain chaos."

Reyson was butt hurt, though in reality they were half right - throw in some Oreos, Starbucks, and a few filthy books and you could keep him occupied for a good long while! I was trying not to laugh because I'd seen him turn someone into a roach for offending him.

"The hedges witches know Dorian wanted Hettie to raise a god, but they don't know why. They are trying to find a way to help so they don't end up getting caught in the crossfire. They are fairly certain she's dead," Balthazar said.

Reyson puffed his chest out.

"She might not have known why, but she had every intention of trying to control me. It was within my rights to turn her into a pest."

"Let's avoid turning the rest of her coven into cockroaches," I said. "If they show up here wanting to help, we can use that. Dorian thinks Reyson is with them. Maybe they can get some information out of Dorian."

"No," Balthazar said, rubbing his nose on my neck

again. "Leave them out of this. They only got involved because they wanted to support a sister witch. They are already scared. Let's not put them in danger."

So far, Balthazar had been all about unleashing Reyson on the world to stop this.

I didn't take him for being sympathetic towards hedge witches at all, especially with that nasty curse on his cock.

"Didn't you say you had a twin sister who worked at the Museum of the Profane?" Gabriel said.

"Yeah, Ravyn. Why?"

"People built elaborate graves back then. You wouldn't entomb a god without pomp, circumstance, and relics there to protect you if he broke out. How do we know Silvaria and Dorian aren't thinking they can control Reyson with something they found in his tomb?"

"Silly superstitious nonsense," Reyson growled.

"No, he's right. They got you in there and kept you there. I need to call my sister and find out if there's anything like that in existence."

"They got me in the tomb because of a woman. She sacrificed herself to get walled up in there with me because they blamed me for something I had nothing to do with. I could have bust out of there and killed every last one of them, but I left Earth for the aether because they didn't deserve my presence in their city."

"I still have to ask, Reyson. Witchcraft has come a long way since then. It might not have existed then, but it might now, and we've got demons involved."

He just let out this little grunt.

"I demand snuggles like the vampire is getting when you get off the phone."

I cocked an eyebrow at him.

"Excuse me? You... demand?"

"Fine. I would *like* to snuggle with you when you get off the phone. I don't mind if everyone else joins."

I rolled over and buried my face in Balthazar's chest. I was trying not to giggle. There was this delicate line between giving Reyson a hard time and getting turned into a cockroach, and I was definitely straddling it; but Balthazar was right. Reyson was trying, and I needed to start doing the same.

"How about you and me have some alone time after dinner?"

Reyson beamed at me and bowed his head.

"Of course, my witch."

"I'm going to my bedroom to call my sister. This needs to be done without comment from the peanut gallery."

I went back to my bedroom and shut the door. I flopped on my bed and pulled out my phone. I couldn't believe I hadn't called Ravyn during all of this. Resurrecting a god was significant and we talked about everything. I guess there was just so much going on that I didn't find the time. I hadn't even texted. I hit her number on speed dial and nestled into my pillow. She picked up on the second ring. Today was her day off, too.

"Bitch, where have you been, and what is his name?" she answered.

"It's complicated, and there are four of them."

"Seriously, Ripley? When are you going to learn? You'll be so much happier when you swear off men all together like I did."

Yeah, my sister and I had the exact same luck with men, just different tastes.

"It's different this time. It involves the cosmos."

"You're a witch, not a shifter. You don't get a fated mate. Are you hitting the Venom? You know how bad that drug is. You—"

My sister got diarrhea of the mouth over literally everything. Sometimes, you just had to be rude and interrupt.

"Ravyn! Will you shut up and listen? Someone came in for necromancy. It wasn't her Uncle Seth she wanted to resurrect, like she told me. No, it was a fucking god! He's here with me. Long story short, there's a warlock with me who keeps drawing the same tarot spread as me, Felix has a body again, and I've got a vampire hacking board members."

The line went totally silent for a good five minutes.

Ravyn sighed. "Are you mixing Venom and booze, Ripley?"

"No! I'm stone-cold sober! Listen to me. Something is about to go down. A bunch of people who made deals with demons wanted a god on their side, so they tricked me into raising Chaos. He's on my side, not theirs. Reyson gave Felix his body back with a flick of his wrist. Some spirits here aren't happy. They made a deal with Silvaria to let Dorian Gray have an all-access library card in exchange for destroying all the Profane buildings and giving them some sort of mass rites.

"It's not all of them. Some of them are trying to help me. I drew the Three of Pentacles, and so did Gabriel. The spirits are trying to help me by giving those people all access cards. I *know* why they are here now. They've proven themselves. Now I need your help."

The line went silent again, and I realized exactly what I sounded like. Ravyn and I had both experimented with Venom at the Academy, and this was precisely the kind of crazy shit someone high on it would come out with.

"You're being totally serious right now, aren't you?"

"Yes! If the board of the library is corrupt then chances are this could come your way at the museum too."

"What can I do to help?"

"Balthazar and Reyson have the means to spy on Silvaria and Dorian. Balthazar is a hacker, and Reyson is a god. We don't know the full story, or how this ties back to Hell, but we know they think they have the ability to control Reyson now that he's back. Does any such relic exist that would give them that power?"

"Different cultures have had them over the ages. We have two on display at the museum. We have no way of knowing if they actually work or not, since everyone is dead, and we obviously can't test them... but both of those relics have something in common. The civilizations they came from were completely exterminated in what you could call very godlike ways. Some of the previous curators thought they worked, but one of the more religious citizens helped the god, and they punished the entire city. Others thought the city went through the trouble of trying to make something that would never work, and the god was outraged that they even tried in the first place. No one knows for sure."

"Reyson turned the hedge witch who brought him into a cockroach for ordering him around, and now when Felix turns into a cat, he has a big dick made out of white fur on his face, just because he knocked over his cookies. Either theory is valid. Reyson thinks they are hocus pocus."

"Are we going to talk about Felix having a body? Did he leave?"

"No, he's still with me. He's hot as fuck, Ravyn."

"*Please* tell me you didn't fuck your familiar."

"I don't kiss and tell."

"Since when? I've heard so many sordid details about your romps. I feel dirty."

That was true. We shared everything, including details about our love lives. Ravyn and Felix used to be the only ones who knew about Dorian and me. I wanted to keep this to myself. That night with Felix and Reyson was different. There were a lot more feelings involved than my usual bedroom antics.

"It was special, Ravyn. I don't want to make it dirty by talking about it."

"Oh, fine. The relics at the museum aren't going to help you with Reyson though. They are both spelled totally differently. The current theory is that whoever wrote the spells on each totem did so with a particular god in mind. I've studied them, and I think that theory is correct. The magic in both totems is like nothing that exists today, but both are so different, which has to be because they were intended to control or neutralize different gods."

"What about the really dangerous grimoires you have at the museum? The ones they won't put out at the library. Is there anything in those about gods?"

"Not according to our catalog. There was recently a dig in Ireland where they unearthed several relics from the Aether Sisters. Remember that coven from our history classes? Their grimoire was found, and it's coming to me, not you. Sorry, not sorry."

"No shit. The Aether Sisters? Keep it. I don't want their evil magic in my library. Their reign of terror was legendary. The entire magical community came together to wipe them out. How'd anyone find their grimoire intact?"

"No one checked under the floor after they burned them alive in their cottage, not until someone was doing some digging at the site. There was an entire cavern underground with the grimoire and some really nasty cursed objects."

My thing was books. It always had been. My twin sister liked to live dangerously and her thing had always been dangerous magical items. I was so happy for her when she got the job at the museum, because it was perfect for her. Receiving objects from one of the most infamous covens in witch history was right up her alley.

"If you find anything in that grimoire, will you let me know?"

"Yeah. When do I get to meet your new harem then?"

"I'm *not* dating them. We're just working together."

Ravyn just laughed.

"Keep telling yourself that, Ripley, but you can't lie to me. You know you will."

I knew I was lying to myself, too. The fact that I hadn't screwed my way through all of them by now and was trying to get to know them first told me I was in deep shit.

CHAPTER 34
RIPLEY

I had absolutely no problem seducing Felix, snuggling with Balthazar and letting him bite me, or inviting Reyson to sleep with Felix and me. What I was super nervous about was being alone in my bed with him after all that, and it didn't make a lick of sense.

I had no problems getting guys in my bed. A little red lipstick, a little flirting, and I could take my pick. That's all it ever was—bedroom romps. I hadn't had a steady boyfriend since the Academy, and even that was a disaster. We got into an argument over something petty—the correct pronunciation of an incantation. He got so mad at me for correcting him then tried to get back at me by taking my twin sister to bed. He might have been a disloyal fuck, but Ravyn wasn't. She kicked him out of our dorm room with a face full of pustules.

Reyson wanted more than that. I would have been more comfortable with it if he had just wanted to fuck. We could have gotten it over with and gone back to work. This? Reyson was trying to romance me, and not in ways I was used to. I was used to cheesy pickup lines and being the aggressor. Reyson fucking cooked me breakfast and didn't ask for sex in return.

I knew I needed to get to know him better, but being alone with him made me nervous.

I STEPPED out of my bedroom and Reyson wasn't in the living room anymore, but something delicious smelling was wafting from the kitchen. Reyson was at my oven again, pulling out a pan. The God of Chaos had fucking baked for me!

"Hello, my witch. I decided to occupy myself while you were speaking with your sister by making my favorite honey cakes. I wanted to show you food from my time, since you've introduced me to yours."

That was actually... sweet. He could have just snapped his fingers and made them appear, but he mixed the ingredients on his own and stuck them in the oven, though I was sure he magicked some ingredients I didn't have. No guy had ever cooked for me before, much less baked a cake for me. Yeah, discomfort level definitely rising!

Reyson set the pan on the table and started slicing the cake for everyone. I decided to share what I'd learned about the relics and the museum and the grimoire that had been found. Everyone had heard of the Aether Sisters, everyone except Reyson. That was after his time. Balthazar would have been taught vampire history, not witch history, but history intertwined with that coven because they didn't discriminate against who they hurt.

"There won't be anything in that grimoire, and

those items at the museum would have been useless. Don't you think witches and warlocks have flung curses at me before? They bounce off me. Vampires and shifters can draw blood, but I instantly heal. The only reason I entered that tomb was that I thought I was bedding a wench. The only reason I left my vessel was that I was done with humanity in general. Nothing on this planet can hurt me or control me."

FELIX AND I SHARED A GLANCE. We didn't have to say anything to each other. Felix and I enjoyed the same type of movies. I got that they were fiction better than anyone in this room, but everyone had a weakness. Gods were all-powerful beings created by the cosmos, but they had to have at least one.

I took a bite of Reyson's cake and moaned. I was so used to cakes with a ton of icing and sugar. Reyson's cake was simple and sweetened with only honey. It was also amazing. Why was he so into Oreos if he could make this?

"Oh, my Lilith! Reyson! This is amazing. You're going to spoil me if you keep cooking for me."

Reyson bowed his head to me.

"It's my goal to spoil you. You should be treated like a goddess, even if you are not as uppity and high maintenance as the other ones I know."

Well, shit. If that was not the sweetest thing anyone had ever said to me. The man made me fucking cake and meat. I really needed to learn everything about him because he was undoubtedly trying harder than anyone else had before.

I finished my cake and brushed the crumbs off my fingers.

"Want to snuggle now, Reyson?"

He was smooth as fuck as he pushed his chair back and tossed his long hair over his shoulder.

"Of course, my witch."

I just went for it. I slipped my hand into his and tugged him to my bedroom. Reyson was the largest man I'd ever met. My hand felt tiny in his.

I felt so small when he was holding me with Felix, but I also felt incredibly safe. Having a god in your bed was probably the most effective alarm system in the Cosmos. He was an excellent snuggler, too.

When we got to my bedroom, I closed the door and walked him back to my bed. He let me shove him onto the bed. He was built like a brick wall. I was guessing shoving or punching him seriously would cause severe damage to whoever tried it, even before he got pissed and struck back.

I hopped into bed and snuggled into his chest. I had been nervous about this and was worried about how weird it would be, but now that I was here, I just felt a wave of serenity settle over me. This was nice.

"Are you doing that?" I sighed.

"Doing what, my witch?"

"Making this feel so good."

"I could, but I've never used my powers on you unless I'm bringing you food. I could *make* you want to marry me, but I won't. I haven't used my powers on any of you, except Felix."

"I never said thank you for making him a full warlock again. Never tell him I said this, but the cock on his face is hilarious."

Reyson let out a rumbling chuckle.

"My lips are sealed, and you're welcome. I should thank you for letting me witness your moment. I apologize for bursting in on you, but I smelled your arousal and couldn't help it."

That should have been so weird, but oddly, it wasn't. Because as soon as he arrived, it got fucking hotter.

"I didn't mind. I enjoyed you watching."

I expected him to bring up joining us or the two of us having sex. Any other guy would. Except Reyson wasn't any other guy. He tightened his arms around me and sighed.

"This is nice."

He was content to just hold me for now, and that was just so bizarre to me.

"Explain the whole god thing to me. What's that like?"

"It is everything at once, but it's also a burden. I didn't get a childhood like you did. I just... was one day. I was a fully formed being instantaneously. There was nothing there then, except a few others like me. Eventually, we started creating and made Earth. We thought it our most incredible creation, and we loved it for a time.

"We loved the adoration and praise people threw our way, but with that came the blame and scorn. Things have to happen to balance the universe. For instance, in a few days, I'm going to have to send a riot to the East to balance the scales. I didn't want to tell you this because I was afraid you would judge me, but I want to be honest with you."

Reyson was something else. He could be a pain in

the ass and a horrible library guest, true, but he was a good guy, even if he was sending a riot somewhere. I craned my head up at him, and his eyes were closed like he was waiting for me to yell at him.

"I get you have duties as a god, Reyson. I'm not angry at you for what you have to do. Do you regret not having a childhood?"

I couldn't imagine what that would be like. He was pretty fascinating. Ravyn would love to pick his brain about all the civilizations he'd seen in the past. Fuck, I wanted to know about those, too.

"I can't say I do since I don't know what it would be like. I know one thing, though. Some of my siblings have had children. Like Gabriel is a descendent of Lucifer, some are descended from my people. I'd like to have children of my own some day."

I couldn't imagine Reyson as a father. I mean, he went around putting dicks on cat's faces and thought fart jokes on television were hilarious. But yeah, maybe I could see it. He'd been nothing but patient and gentle with me thus far.

"Will you have to leave when you cause the riot in the East?"

Reyson just smirked.

"Why? Will you miss me, my witch?"

I swatted at his chest. Yeah, actually, I would. He was growing on me. His chest made such a pleasant rumble when he chuckled. He started tickling me! I shrieked and tried to fight him off.

"I think you will miss me, my witch," he growled, his fingers flying up and down my ribs.

"Yes! Yes, I'll miss you!" I hollered as I tried to catch my breath.

Reyson immediately let me go and pulled me to his chest.

"Well, that was all you had to say."

"Dick."

"Did you want to touch it? I didn't think you were ready for that, but I won't complain."

I actually kind of did. I saw it through his trousers when he kicked the door in.

A girl could have a good time with that, but I didn't want to rush this and ruin it. I could have a good thing with Reyson. I could have a good thing with all of them. Gabriel wasn't overtly hitting on me, but I liked him. I nuzzled my face on Reyson's chest.

"Can we just take things slowly?"

He started petting my hair. If I could have purred like Felix was still doing now that he was a man, I totally would have.

"We can do whatever you want and no, I don't have to leave here to do anything. Your people call it astral projection, though it's a little different for me. I hope to get more information on Dorian tomorrow. Oh, and someone will come tomorrow that has information. I can feel their putrid soul growing closer."

I knew Gabriel and Balthazar were all about unleashing Reyson and letting him do his thing with getting information. Still, there were enough spirits at the Library of the Profane without stacking up a bigger body count.

"Let's avoid killing them if we can," I said.

Reyson just sighed and continued to pet my hair.

"You've got Chaos, Ripley. You might as well use me."

I planned on it. But only when the time was right.

CHAPTER 35
RIPLEY

My bed was full that night. Felix might used to have been a large tomcat but he always started on the pillow on the other side of my bed and somehow ended up in the center. Yeah, my cat used to hog the bed and I'd fallen out as a result few times! I used my magic to conjure up this massive king-sized bed so Felix could monopolize it without kicking me entirely out.

Felix had a human body now, and Reyson had a permanent invitation to snuggle at night. Reyson saw there was plenty of room and thought I should invite Balthazar, since he saw us snuggling on the sectional. Then, it just felt weird to invite Balthazar and not Gabriel, even if it was awkward to go ask him since he wasn't super forward with his flirting like Balthazar was and he hadn't informed me, I was going to marry him like Reyson had done.

Still, they had all agreed with it. Balthazar was happy as a clam to sleep spooning Reyson. Felix insisted Gabriel sleep next to me that night. They smashed me between hot male flesh, and I was quite content. I had to keep reminding myself I didn't want to ruin this by fucking all of them.

This was so ass-backward, too. There always seemed to be more witches than warlocks at any given time. There were female-only covens that would take warlock lovers but never any male-only covens.

It was pretty standard in the witching community for several witches to share one warlock. This right here? Me sharing a bed with two warlocks, a vampire, and a god? That was straight-up shifter shit. I was so here for it though! Those witches who insisted on sharing one man instead of making a man share them had *no idea* what they were missing. All we did all night was snuggle.

We made it a point to get up and down to the library pretty early. Reyson could sense someone who knew something was making their way to us. At least it was just one instead of an entire line of them outside my library this time.

We were all dying to get ahold of them, but we needed to play it cool, or whoever it was would bolt. I would count a god and a vampire leaving face marks on my glass very creepy, and whoever walked up was going to think that, too. I had to grab them by the arms and move them away from the glass at the front.

"If we're going to snatch this person and bring them to the atrium, we can't tip them off until they get inside. We aren't breaking my library, remember? We need to coax them into the atrium, where it's safe to fling magic around if something goes wrong."

"Remind me, why are we being nice to this person again?" Balthazar said. "Just let Reyson knock them out and drag them there. Fuck, I'll punch them in the face and get them here!"

"I'm not exactly inclined to be nice to them either," Gabriel said. "They wanted a god. I say we let them meet him."

I crossed my arms and glared at both of them. We *were not* unleashing Chaos in my library.

"My library, my rules. Reyson can come out to play when it makes sense."

Felix was looking out the window like a sane person.

"It better make sense soon, because there's a warlock headed this way, and his aura is almost entirely black."

Well, fuck. Black auras were never a good sign. Most people didn't walk around with those, they were generally dead or in jail. I had a feeling the reason this one was just strolling up to my library had something to do with a deal he'd made with a demon. Those angry spirits here wouldn't have been dumb enough to cheat him into the library, right? I'd never seen him before, but I didn't know everyone with a library card.

I wanted everything to look totally natural when he came in, but we were all just standing in the foyer, discussing his gross aura. Balthazar was complaining he could smell the stink of his blood from inside. We looked like a bunch of kids with our hands in the candy drawer when the warlock strolled in. Seriously, it was fucking awkward. We all just stopped talking and gawked at him. Balthazar put his hand over his nose like he couldn't deal with the stench. The warlock just glared at us.

"So, I don't have a library card, and I don't want

one. I think every single building on this site is for uppity, pretentious assholes and I feel dirty just setting foot here. So, which one of you assholes is responsible for summoning me here?!"

"You know what?" I said. "We're doing this another way."

I cocked back my fist and punched him in the face. *No one* insulted my library. I quickly realized that I should have hit him with magic because it hurt my hand like hell, but I'd never wanted to hit someone that badly before.

He stumbled backward and flung a curse at me. Felix tackled me to the ground and it just narrowly missed hitting me in the face.

Gabriel flicked his wrists, and ropes bound the warlock's hands. Balthazar tackled him, and they both crashed into this expensive vase that was in the foyer. Fuck. That thing was ugly as fuck. I hated it, but it was centuries old and the board felt the need to put it on display here, so it must be valuable. I hoped they wouldn't take that out of my paycheck.

The warlock broke the ropes and had Balthazar by the neck, holding him at arm's length to keep his fangs away from him. His mouth was still free to chant. I heard the incantation he was trying to utter, and it was forbidden, even in times of war. I tried to call for someone to knock him out before he could finish, but it sucked all the air out of my lungs. I couldn't breathe anymore.

I fell to my knees, clutching my throat. We were all similarly helpless, except Reyson. He must have been right about witch magic not affecting him. He walked straight over to the warlock and kicked him in the head.

The warlock went limp, and I gulped air as it returned to my lungs.

Reyson slung him over his shoulder as we all struggled to get to our feet. Balthazar had a black eye forming, and the vase had cut his cheek. He had accelerated healing as a vampire, and the wound was already knitting itself closed, but he had blood running down his cheek.

"That went well," Balthazar said, brushing his trousers off.

Reyson was looking at me in total adoration.

"Ripley you are quite the warrior. It was an enormous turn on watching you beat on that warlock, my witch."

"You know what? He pissed me off. Balthazar and Gabriel are right. Reyson needs to have a little fun with this one."

Felix slipped his hand in mine.

"Are you sure? Do you really want his spirit here when this is over?"

"He doesn't deserve it, but we can give him the rites and bury him in the garden. I don't want him or his spirit lingering here any longer than necessary."

Felix lifted my bruised knuckles to his lips and kissed them.

"Then, I support you."

Reyson bounced the warlock on his shoulder impatiently.

"Let's get this thing to the atrium. I don't like the way his soul feels. The sooner I get the information out of him, the sooner we don't have to deal with him anymore."

I used to be all about using magic responsibly. I'd

used it to defend myself, but never to kill and never to gain anything I didn't need. My, how I'd changed. The truth potion would have technically gotten the job done, unless his deal with the demon had some sort of immunity to it. I didn't trust that it didn't with his aura being as dark as it was. So I settled on letting Reyson do it his way, knowing it would kill the warlock.

CHAPTER 36
REYSON

I flung the filthy warlock onto one of the chairs in the atrium. Felix snapped his fingers and bound him with way more rope than was necessary. Gabriel conjured a roll of something silver and placed it over the warlock's mouth. We didn't need him doing any more nasty incantations to hurt anyone in the room. The likelihood of him waking before I was done was slim. I held back when I kicked him just enough not to kill him, but hard enough to make my point. He tried to kill my witch.

First things first. Ripley was absolutely magnificent, punching him in the face like that. His lip was busted open, but she cut her knuckles on his teeth. I could not abide by that, even if I were proud of her for taking her vengeance.

I ignored the nasty warlock and walked over to my witch. This could wait two seconds. Felix had already kissed her bruised and bleeding knuckles, but I could do better and heal her. I brushed my lips over her knuckles and watched the shock pass over her face. I told her I'd never use my magic on her. I intended to keep that promise, but I'd make an exception when it came to healing her.

She flexed her hand in front of her face, then flung herself at me. Before I knew it, she was kissing me. If I had known healing her would get her tongue down my throat, I would have scanned her for simple body aches and done away with them.

She tasted amazing. Her magic mingled pleasantly with mine. I wanted to keep doing this. I wanted to carry her back to her bedroom and ravage her. But I restrained myself. Baby steps for now. We had to deal with this warlock. I set her down and tucked one of her black curls behind her ears. She caressed my cheek and looked up at me so fondly. Progress.

"We all would have died back there if it weren't for you. That spell is forbidden."

"I'd never let any of you die. Now, back to this warlock. He's a despicable, dangerous man. His soul is heavily tainted, and it's more than just his deals with demons."

"Probably worse than my relative was, and this fucker isn't even in jail."

I hadn't touched him yet, but I knew why.

"A soul doesn't get this dark without some sort of intervention. Sometimes, my family would protect dark souls like this for a time because we needed them. But you can bet when they were no longer needed we got rid of them. Even with my family's protection, we never allowed a soul to get this black. This is a severe case of demonic influence. He made a very evil deal."

"Yeah, we don't need to see his soul to know that.

We can see his aura, and it's just as black. I don't like being in the same room with him. Can we get this over with?" Gabriel said.

Felix shuddered and glared at the man tied to the chair. Out of all of us, he was the least okay with what I was going to do. He wanted to use his potion, and the only reason he was okay with me using my methods was because Ripley was. Or, maybe not.

"THE VIBE IS JUST off with him in here. Even if his deal was to evade being captured, I don't understand how anyone could stand being in the same room with him without ending him. Do your god thing, Reyson."

I didn't want to lay a finger on this warlock. It wasn't just that his soul was so tainted, his physical body was greasy and unwashed. His hair was unkempt and oily. I could smell his body odor over the wretched stench of his soul. The last time I walked this earth, there wasn't this obsession with bathing like there was in this century, and somehow people back then were still cleaner than this warlock. Gross. Ripley had a bathtub with jets in her apartment, that I could soak in it all day.

Still, I had to touch him to do this. I tried to avoid his greasy hair because it was especially dirty, it wouldn't shock me if it were infested with lice. I laid my palm on his forehead and his entire body tensed.

I saw everything in a matter of minutes. He was thorough when he made his deal. He would never be caught or killed until his payment came due. This warlock had gotten up to some evil shit. He knew it, too. He knew it was only a matter of time before the demon he made a deal with came to collect payment.

When he heard a rumor there was a way to get out of his deal, but still keep the perks, he jumped at it. He never met with Silvaria or Dorian directly, but word spread in the magical community amongst those who made deals in secret.

There was a way to get out of the deal and keep your soul. You could stiff the demon on payment and keep everything they offered you.

I LET GO OF HIM. I'd seen everything there was to see, and his brains were leaking out of his ears. I knew why Silvaria and Dorian went through the trouble to bring me back, and we had an enormous problem.

"Silvaria and Dorian think I can break their contracts with Hell but let them keep their gifts. This warlock hasn't even met them. Word is spreading among the magical community that there's a way out. Silvaria and Dorian are building an army. This isn't good. When Hell hears about this, they will send their own military and start collecting payments.

"I can't break a Hell contract, but Silvaria and Dorian have no way of knowing that. I could kill demons if I needed to, but they tend to take that personally. If any of Silvaria and Dorian's people kill a demon, or we do, they will attack this entire planet. That Hellhound needs to get his ass back on Earth so I can get him at the library. I suspect he's one of us."

Gabriel just frowned.

"Aren't demons and Hellhounds bad? Shouldn't we be avoiding them?"

An easy assumption to make. I wouldn't say I liked them, but they were doing what people had been since my family created them.

"They aren't bad, per se. They are business people, and their currency is souls. I don't know what they do with them in Hell, but they provide a service in exchange for that currency, just like people have been doing since the dawn of time. They'd stop coming if there weren't a market for what they are offering. You saw the number of people outside the library. It's more common than you think it is. It's just that people don't talk about it.

"When payment is collected, it looks like natural causes, so the secret never gets out, not unless the person who made the deal tells someone or does something stupid to try to get out of their contract."

Poor Gabriel looked so confused. I knew his lot in life had to do with an ancestor who made a deal ages ago, but it would never have been public knowledge unless the deal was for something awful and they went out of their way to break the contract. People died horribly if they defaulted on their payment. There were telltale signs the death was demonic.

He looked like he didn't know what to say, and I didn't know how to make this better for him. I couldn't change how people treated him. I could only treat him with kindness and respect. He didn't deserve anything that happened to him just because of his family.

Gabriel changed the subject.

"This warlock stinks of body odor and evil. And it's gross the way his brains are leaking out of him like that. Can we hurry up and do the rites and bury him? I don't want his spirit lurking around here."

We got our information, and I tried to do all I could to avoid an all-out war with Hell. But I'd just taken a soul due to a demon, so someone was going to come asking questions.

I just hoped it was this Bram and not an enemy.

CHAPTER 37
BRAM

I needed to be back on Earth, but I was stuck in Hell waiting for a seer to have a vision. My master had gone to collect Dorian Gray's payment. The pretty playboy had a long, decadent life. He'd seen way more than the average human would ever see. He'd experienced several centuries' worth of life. It was high time for his payment to be due.

My master was fair and kind. He bought me when I was just a pup and trained me to be a soldier. He never beat me like some of the other demons beat their Hellhounds. He let me come and go as I pleased, that is unless he needed me for something. Talvath usually collected his own payments unless he was on vacation. He'd send me when he was kicking his heels up on the beach. Talvath knew I enjoyed Earth, so he let me take my time collecting the soul, and I didn't have to hurry back with it.

But something went wrong when he went to collect Dorian Gray's payment. Something went horribly wrong. Since someone made the first deal with us, they fought about making their payment when it was due. There were too many rumors about how Hell was supposed to be this place of eternal torment for souls that ended up here.

We didn't torture anyone. The souls we collected powered our sun. This was ages before I was ever born, but Hell was dying. Our sun was dying, and crops wouldn't grow.

Demons went to Earth to try to find a solution. They found that the beings there seemed to radiate with the same energy as our dying sun, but they couldn't just take their souls. Their universe was protected by its own deities, just like Hell was.

A very entrepreneurial demon came up with a solution the gods couldn't argue with. She turned it into a business transaction. A demon would grant something that a person asked for and, in turn, Hell would get their soul. People ate it up, even if they didn't know what Hell was really like.

Some people fought making their payment, but they never won. Their souls were harvested and brought back to Hell to power our sun. Something went wrong when Talvath went to collect Dorian's payment though, he should have been back by now. He liked to dally on Earth just as much as I did, but he'd never been gone this long.

It wasn't like he was up there partying with Dorian either. Talvath talked to me like I was an actual person instead of his pet. He didn't like Dorian. Dorian wasn't the one who summoned him, it was a witch. Talvath didn't like that Dorian didn't do any of the work and that what he asked for was so vapid and self-centered.

He granted it because a soul was a soul, but he really didn't like Dorian.

I went to Earth to find my master and spy on Dorian Gray. Talvath was nowhere to be found, and that was frightening. No one on Earth was supposed to possess the knowledge to kill a demon. Many had tried, and none succeeded. Demons granted almost every deal, but they wouldn't have given out that ability freely.

Dorian was up to something. I saw him meeting with two women. One was a haughty woman, whose payment would come due soon, and the other a plain looking hedge witch who was head over heels in love with him.

I followed him to the Library of the Profane. We knew of it, even in Hell. We had our own libraries there, but we weren't so stingy with knowledge like they were on Earth. Anyone could access ours. I knew the library had this vetting process and shouldn't have allowed anyone who was demon tainted access to their books, even if it was a deal for something as innocently vapid as vanity.

I needed to see what he was researching, so I strolled in and applied for a card. I didn't think I'd be granted a card, given that I was a Hell pet. I don't know who was more surprised—that insanely hot librarian or me. Hell librarians were nowhere near that sexy.

Dorian was looking up gods, and that didn't bode well for Hell. Demons only feared one thing on Earth, the gods. Yeah, they may have gotten a little lax with granting nearly everything that was asked because the gods were all gone. He was explicitly researching summoning them back.

One in particular. The God of Chaos. I read what Dorian read about him. He'd gone by many names throughout history and was generally feared by everyone. They had tricked him into a tomb and he'd then disappeared. We did not need Dorian summoning Chaos to get out of his payment. And how had a human killed Talvath?

Just like that, Dorian stopped going to the library. He abandoned his research and flew to Paris. He seemed to try to form alliances with several people who had made deals. I could kill Dorian easily and bring his soul back to Hell.

Something bigger was going on. Talvath was missing, and Dorian was amassing an army.

It looked like he wanted a god to head it. So, there I was, back in Hell visiting with Talvath's seer.

Visions couldn't be forced and I was just sitting around doing nothing while Dorian had time to gather more people and possibly raise a god. Hell was vast, but I already knew how this was going to play out. Hellhounds were soldiers. We would be the ones sent to die in this war.

They had separated me from my siblings when I was just a pup. I didn't know them as an adult. But I was friends with a lot of Hellhounds. A lot of us were beaten, abused, and treated as expendable. Demons wouldn't go out and fight a god if Dorian succeeded. They would send their pets. I needed to stop it before it got that bad.

Anod, Talvath's seer, burst into my bedroom.

"A vision came."

"Did you find Talvath?"

"No. You have allies. You need to go back to the

Library of the Profane. The librarian there is a friend, and she's called help to her side. You're a part of that. The god is with her, and he's a friend. They can help you stop this before it becomes an all-out war."

"Does killing Dorian Gray stop this?"

"Not anymore. He has his own allies, and he's been making promises he can't keep. You need to find his painting."

I nodded. Next stop—the Library of the Profane. I wouldn't mind making friends with that sexy librarian while I was there.

CHAPTER 38
RIPLEY

I usually loved my job, but it seemed so fucked up to be sitting at work while Dorian and Silvaria built an army to provoke a war with Hell. Still, we had more resources here than anywhere else. Felix, Gabriel, and I were reading every book on demons the library had. Balthazar had his laptop out, trying to figure out Silvaria's next move. Meanwhile Reyson was spying on Dorian and trying to find Bram. Hell was apparently off-limits to Gods.

Demon lore was hazy at best. There were several theories about how to contain one for a period of time, but I doubted those actually worked, or more people would be bragging about getting out of their deals, and we wouldn't be in this mess with Dorian in the first place!

Reyson finally jumped up and hollered. This was a quiet place, and we all jumped. I shushed him out of instinct.

"The Hellhound has left Hell! Give me ten minutes, and I can contact him."

Reyson didn't even get that chance. Bram walked in the front door then and strolled right up to my desk with a smirk on his face.

"Man, was I sure glad when the seer told me to come back here and look at that pretty face again."

"Took you long enough," Reyson boomed. "I've been trying to find you for days."

"You must be the god. Bram."

"Reyson. Is there any reason you spent so long in Hell when Dorian and Silvaria are up to no good?"

"Waiting for a seer to have a vision. My master went to collect Dorian's soul. He's missing. No one here should have the ability to kill a demon. It takes a special weapon that you can only get in Hell, and no demon would trade that away in a deal. I don't think Talvath is dead, but I can't sense him anywhere. The seer told me to come to the Library of the Profane, and I would find help."

Well, this was the perfect place. We had all these books, Dorian's painting, and a god to help figure this all out. I wanted to help Bram in any way I could, but I didn't particularly want to find his master so he could go back to being a slave. Still, I'd have to, so we could stop Dorian.

I grabbed a chair and pulled it up to my desk. I patted the seat for Bram to join us.

"We've been looking at books on demon lore. Some of these books have theories that cover trapping demons, but I don't think any of them actually work. Can you look at these books and tell me if any of these runes and incantations would successfully trap a demon? It may help us find your master."

Balthazar was still glued to his laptop. Reyson had

gone back into his trance, probably to watch Dorian this time.

"If Silvaria is hiding a demon, I think I know where," Balthazar said. "She's got a storage container that was built on an old Native American gravesite. Capitalism, right?"

"She's been sending emails every day to this warlock to make sure he's checked on the contents. If there's a demon in there, he probably needs to eat."

"Let's go get him!" Bram said.

"Hold up there, Sparky," Gabriel said. "Silvaria has made a deal with a demon. If she's figured out how to keep a demon hostage, there are probably some really nasty magical booby traps to make sure no one gets in that isn't supposed to. I'm not talking about curses either. Silvaria is going down a dark road, probably one of evil, killing magic."

Shit. He was right. I watched the warlock's magic bounce right off Reyson, but if Bram's master was missing, then anything could be possible. That meant Silvaria could have found a spell to trap Reyson, too. I needed to think.

"Do you see anything in these books that would make it possible to contain a demon?" Felix asked.

Bram bit down on his lip ring.

"Not on their own. But if you combined bits and pieces from four of these pages, it could work, but the odds of figuring that out without getting killed would be... slim, at best."

"It would really help if Silvaria were one of those dumbasses who digitized their grimoire," Balthazar said. "Or if she was giving out her information online instead of in person."

"Now that Bram is here, I can watch Silvaria and Dorian," Reyson said.

I saw this lightbulb go off over Reyson's head and his entire face lit up.

"Bram, you're a shifter, right? Kind of like a wolf?"

I jumped across my desk and clapped my hand over his mouth. I knew exactly where this was going.

"Bram just got here. Let's not scare him off."

"I'm far superior to a wolf, but I don't have the same freedom."

Reyson was trying to talk around my hand, and I glared at him.

"Don't you dare!"

"Is there something you aren't telling me?" Bram asked.

Felix snorted.

"Reyson is super curious about shifter cock."

Of course, my familiar had to betray me. I was mortified. Bram *just* got here, and now everyone wanted to know about his dick! Bram certainly wasn't embarrassed. He puffed out his chest and adjusted his crotch.

"It's pierced, and I've got the knot."

Balthazar and Reyson let out a little groan. Fuck. *I* let out a small moan. Bram was just smirking at us because we were all panting at the idea of his cock. His hand went to his fly.

"Want to see?"

My hand was still clamped over Reyson's mouth. Reyson nodded enthusiastically. Balthazar just flashed his fangs and grinned. I scowled. This was *not* happening in my library.

"*Do not* take your dick out in *my* library!"

Bram just shrugged. Gabriel rolled his eyes.

"Now that's out of the way, can we get back to the demons and Bram's master?" Gabriel said.

"Silvaria just emailed Dorian. They are both feeling the pull to the library. They are certain it's Reyson. Silvaria thinks Ripley is some idiot who is keeping him safe until she can come to claim him. How did this witch get to be on the board?! She's the queen of stupidity!"

That was the problem. Silvaria was vapid, but she certainly wasn't stupid. She was pretty damned cunning. This whole thing, her thinking she could control Reyson was dumb... unless she knew something we didn't. We just learned someone had pieced together runes to trap a demon.

Reyson said nothing existed that could control him. Bram thought the same thing about what people knew here on Earth. But, clearly, someone had managed if Talvath was missing.

"We need a game plan," I announced.

"We need to rescue Talvath," Bram said.

"We can't do that until we figure out the wards and spells on that storage container," Felix said.

"Then we need to take Dorian out of the equation," Bram said. "Talvath was here for Dorian's soul. I can take Dorian's soul, and this Silvaria will have to plot without him. I just need to find his painting. Talvath put his soul in the painting to make him immortal."

I grinned. Things were falling into place.

"I've got the painting right here in the vaults of the library."

Dorian Gray was going down.

CHAPTER 39
BALTHAZAR

I didn't particularly want to look at that nasty painting. The idea of ripping my soul out and stashing it in a picture so I could be pretty for a long time was an abomination to me. There was a lot of beauty in wrinkles that so many people didn't appreciate.

I was off on a scouting mission. Felix was riding bitch on my motorcycle because I needed a witch for this. I knew he didn't want to leave Ripley behind, but he was a kinky little cat. He was letting her get to know Gabriel and Bram better by giving them space. I dug it, but I wanted time with her, too. I got my snuggle time with Reyson, and it was all I could do not to bite him. I wanted sleep spooning with Ripley next.

The storage site was way out of the way. It honestly never should have been built. Someone clearly had to grease some palms to get it built on a Native American burial site, but people had been fucking those people over since they first landed on these shores, so it didn't surprise me.

I got bad vibes from the place when I parked my bike. I broke out in goosebumps, and my fangs tingled like a fight was coming. Felix hopped off my bike and stood next to me.

"This must be where a lot of witches and warlocks are storing things too dangerous to keep in their houses. This place reeks of dark magic. One call to Ravyn and everything here would be destroyed or locked up at the Museum of the Profane."

I hissed. I hated it here already.

"Silvaria's container is all the way in the back. We're going to have to trudge through these dank vibes to get to it."

"I'm going to change into the cat. Can you put my clothes in your gear bag, so they don't get dirty?"

"Of course."

I knew Felix had been Ripley's familiar until Reyson gave him his body back, but I'd never seen him as the cat before. I'd never seen him change. It differed so much to how shifters changed. I didn't hear his bones snapping, and it was all over pretty quickly. A black tomcat crawled out of Felix's trousers. I stared at the cat.

"Is that a cock on your face?"

Felix hissed and swatted at my shins. I jumped back because I didn't mess with cats. They used to be worshipped as gods for a reason! Clearly, he was sensitive about the big white dick on his face. I wondered if Reyson was responsible for that, too.

We made our way down corridors of storage containers. My feelings of unease grew with each step. Even if there wasn't a demon hidden somewhere in here, people were storing some nasty shit in these containers. I was about ready to jump straight out of my skin by the time we got to Silvaria's.

I looked down at the cat. I couldn't talk to Felix like this, but we didn't need to. Silvaria had a guard posted outside her container. I couldn't get close, but Felix could. I could see with my enhanced vision that Silvaria didn't just have a guard at the door. She had an enchanted lock.

You could buy those at any witch shop, and I had a few of those of my own. They didn't use keys or combinations, but required blood, and only that specific blood would open it. If you pricked your finger on the lock and you weren't supposed to, it didn't just not open for you. It left a little hex behind in your blood, and, depending on the witch, it could simply be a nuisance or fatal. I guessed this lock was deadly, so that big ass shifter pacing in front of the door was just overkill.

He looked like a grumpy ass mother fucker. I could smell his putrid blood from here. Sulfur. Another one who'd made a deal. He had this look on his face like he hated every minute of being out there, but I could smell fear on him, too. Endorphins were surging through his veins that should have triggered a fight or flight response, but something was keeping him here.

The storage container was airtight, but ventilated. I could smell it. Everyone that was demon tainted reeked of sulphur and smelled nasty. Bram was from Hell, and he didn't somehow. His blood smelled terrific. It was unlike anything I'd ever smelled before. It reminded me of roasting marshmallows over a campfire on a perfect night.

There was *someone* inside the storage container. I

could hear the extra heartbeat. I had accounted for Felix and the shifter, but this extra heartbeat was weakened and faint, precisely like someone who was being contained and having their powers dampened.

I'd confirmed someone was being held inside the storage container. Felix would have seen the blood lock. Based on the blood lock and the guard, I didn't think those were the only precautions Silvaria had taken to secure this storage container.

No one had ever successfully held a demon hostage before. She probably had the place full of wards and cursed objects to kill anyone who wasn't allowed inside. I knew we needed to free whoever was in there, but I didn't know how without getting killed.

Our best bet was Reyson. He was sure nothing on this planet could control him or hurt him. But we had all been sure demons couldn't be controlled either, until Bram's slave master went missing.

Felix came slinking back to where I was hiding, and we made it back to my motorcycle. He changed back into a man, and I handed him his clothes. I peeked first, of course. Felix was a gorgeous man, and I had a healthy appreciation for that.

Felix pulled his zipper up and stared at me.

"Shifting makes me hungry. I think I want to try Taco Bell. Ripley and Ravyn would stop there at two in the morning in college."

"You've never had Taco Bell?"

"I've never had Mexican food. It wasn't available in London when I was alive."

I grinned at him. He was like my own little alien to show the world.

"Well, your first experience with Mexican food is going to be authentic. I'm not taking you to Taco Bell. Hop on. This is a job for Pablo."

Pablo was a vampire from Mexico. He'd immigrated to the US when he was seventeen. His Abuela made the best food in the entire world, and she taught him everything she knew. I ate with his family when I was in town for work, and he'd be eating right about now.

People were constantly dropping by his table, and he wouldn't think it was weird for me to just show up unannounced with Felix.

We needed to discuss what we learned at the storage yard, but we could do that in front of Pablo. I trusted him with my life, and he'd gotten me out of a few severe binds before. Pablo was also the sanest person I knew, and if anyone could give us advice, it would be him. I liked every single person I was now joined with at the library, but we weren't exactly a sane bunch.

I pulled my bike down the dirt road to Pablo's mobile home. I knocked the kickstand down and hopped off. Felix pulled his helmet off and raised an eyebrow at me.

"This is *not* a restaurant, Balthazar."

"No, but it's the best Mexican food in the state."

"You're just going to barge in on some poor schlep and demand he feeds us?"

"I'll bet you the right to snuggle next to Ripley for three whole days the food is ready, there's enough for both of us, and that Pablo treats you like his brother."

"You're one horny wanker, Balthazar. I'm not

taking that bet. We need to compare notes about what we found in the storage yard. We should leave."

I just clapped him on the back.

"We can do that here."

I started walking towards the trailer. He could either sit out here and starve, or follow me. I could smell something beautiful involving steak, even from all the way out here. Felix could, too, because he was following me, even if he was bitching about it.

Pablo flung the door open before I could knock. Being a vampire was like having a built in alarm system. We would hear your heartbeat well before you ever got inside. It was different for everyone, but Pablo would have known a vampire and a witch were out here, and he had no enemies.

"Balthazar!" he cried, pulling me into a hug. "Are you in trouble again?"

"Something like that, but that's not why I'm here. This one has never had Mexican food before, and he wanted to start with Taco Bell."

"That hurts my feelings," Pablo said with his hand over his heart. "Get your asses in here and eat."

I gave Felix an *I told you so* look and went to the dining room to eat. Pablo always cooked massive amounts of food because people turned up to eat all the time. It was just us today, and for that, I was glad. We needed to talk about that cargo yard, and Pablo was the only person I trusted enough to do so in front of.

"Someone was inside that shipping container," I said as I dug into my food.

Felix hadn't even touched his, and he tried to shush me. I waved my fork at him.

"Pablo is a priest. He hears this shit all the time. He

won't tell anyone. He's studied everything there is to know about Nosferatu. He might have some insights on Reyson and demons."

"Not *exactly* this shit. You should have said that before we came inside."

"I'm getting offended you haven't eaten yet," Pablo said. "Why don't you take a bite and tell me what the problem is?"

Felix finally ate his damned food after all that bitching about Taco Bell.

"Do you know anything about controlling gods?"

"Many have tried, and they all met horrible ends."

"Oh, my Lilith! This is amazing," Felix moaned.

Pablo just rolled his eyes.

"Finally. If you had preferred Taco Bell to my Abuela's secret recipe, I was going to have to pray hard for you."

"We just found out someone may have found a way to trap a demon. The people who trapped him have raised the God of Chaos. He's on our side, and wants to punish these people, but they are acting like they are certain they have a way to control him."

Pablo's eyebrows raised to his forehead.

"You do manage to get yourself into the most complicated of shit, Balthazar. Out of all the gods to raise, I'd be asking yourselves this, why Chaos? No one worships him anymore. Depending on who did it, I would expect to see Lilith, Nosferatu, or one of the various shifter gods. Why raise someone you haven't spent your entire life paying tribute to? Especially Chaos. He was generally feared since he was so unpredictable."

Reyson seemed pretty reasonable to me. He cared

about Ripley, food, and killing anyone who thought they could control him. He was also being super careful with how he dealt with this, because any wrong move would bring an army of demons here. Still, I couldn't deny he could be dangerous if he wanted to be. He was the god of fucking Chaos, after all.

"They are all trying to get out of deals they made with demons," Felix said. "They think he will break their contracts or kill the demons who own them, but still somehow allow them to keep the gifts the demons gave them. They seemed pretty sure they could get him to do it."

"We've all met him and spent time with him," I said. "He wouldn't do that just for the hell of it. I know he's Chaos personified, but he takes his powers seriously."

"Unless you bat his Oreos over because you're a cat," Felix muttered.

I almost fell out of my chair laughing.

"Is that how you got a dick on your face?"

Felix pointed his steak knife at me.

"I'd appreciate you *never* mentioning that to my face ever again."

"That's the thing," Pablo said. "Most of the gods wouldn't abuse their power like that. If I had to pick any god who would help them, it would be Chaos, or a trickster god. But the risks are too great with both. A trickster is liable to run off and do their own thing, and Chaos is one of the original gods. He helped create the universe. He could either take offense at demon deals, or he could have been part of the creation of demons."

It was exceptionally fucking rare that I knew something Pablo didn't. I met him at church. Though I wasn't super religious and didn't really attend, I'd stumbled through his door once, all broken and bloodied and asking for sanctuary because some vampires I hacked were trying to rip my head off. That was how we met, became friends, and I found out his Abuela was a genius in the kitchen.

"Gods and demons are totally separate. We met a Hellhound too. Gods can't go to Hell, and demons fear gods."

"You certainly have been on an adventure."

"We need to talk about that storage container," Felix said.

"There's someone in there," I said. "I could hear their heartbeat. It was faint, like their magic was being tampered with. I saw the blood lock, too. The shifter guarding the door has clearly made a deal. He reeked of sulphur."

"I figured as much. The storage yard isn't just on a burial ground. Silvaria's container is on a ley line. She's got some seriously dangerous objects in there, and I sensed a lot of blood."

"Oh, yeah. She's got all kinds of blood in there. I smelled witch, vampire, human, and all kinds of shifter. She's got her bases well and truly covered."

"Bits and pieces! Bram said bits and pieces from those books would work. One binding ritual said the blood of all races would bind the demon, and the other said drawing the rune in blood would bind them. I'll bet she drew it in the blood of everyone. She must have been preparing for this for ages."

Pablo pulled out a bottle of tequila and poured it

into three shot glasses. He slid them across the table and downed his.

"I don't suppose I can talk you into sitting this one out?"

"You know me. I have to stop the end of the world."

"Thank you for the food, Pablo," Felix said. "It was truly amazing, and I'm glad I had your Abuela's recipes for my first time eating Mexican food."

Pablo just grinned.

"Good. Now, swear to me you'll never eat Taco Bell."

"Can I bring Ripley here, so *she'll* stop eating Taco Bell?"

"If she comes, Reyson will tag along. You'll get to meet a god, Pablo."

"You know my table is always open, Balthazar. I look forward to meeting your new family. Now, go stop the end of the world and try not to get killed!"

It was time to get back. Dorian Gray should be good and dead by now. It was time to report back what we learned about Silvaria. Personally, I thought we should only free this demon if he agreed to grant Bram his freedom, but that was just me.

Slavery had never been cool.

CHAPTER 40
RIPLEY

It made sense to split into teams since our numbers had grown. I didn't like the idea of Felix or Balthazar going off to a storage yard built on a gravesite alone, but I knew they were both capable, so I would just have to deal with it. I was on painting duty with Gabriel, Reyson, and Bram.

I realized the level of hot shit I'd be in if I destroyed this painting while it was in my care. I had no legally obtained proof against Silvaria. The spirits here at the library seemed willing to help me, but would they cooperate if anyone else summoned them? The only reason they really did so for us was because Reyson made them his little bitch.

I couldn't be in there with them because I had to work. I could get fired for that, too. I unlocked the vault on my lunch break and let Reyson, Gabriel, and Bram inside.

"*Do not* break anything in here. Deal with the painting and get out. We keep our sentient books in here. Try not to be loud, or they will attack you. Please, do not damage these books. If you need more space then move the painting to my apartment and deal with it there."

"It's going to get messy, so I'll move it," Bram said.

I didn't know the first thing about harvesting a soul from a painting, but if it made a mess, they had better not do it in the vault and clean up after themselves afterward.

I didn't want to leave, but I went back to my desk. A face I really wanted to see strolled up to my desk to return a book. I needed to pick Professor Krauss' brain about Balthazar's curse.

"Hi, Professor Krauss. Can I ask you a few questions about curses?"

"Dear, haven't I asked you to call me Minerva now that you aren't my student anymore?"

Yeah, she had asked. Probably a million times, but it was just so fucking embarrassing. I was terrified of this woman when she was my teacher.

"Sorry. Old habits. Did you like the book?"

"You were right about the pack dynamics in this one. Any news about when the next one is coming out?"

"It's not up for pre-order yet, and it hasn't been announced, but book four is coming out as an audiobook in three weeks. Dirk Berghan is back for the lead. His voice does things to me."

"Do you have any tea and any more of those lovely cookies? I know we usually discuss books, but I'd be happy to talk curses with you, dear."

I always kept lemon macrons on hand because they were her favorite. You could only drink tea in the atrium or at my desk, but there was a pot available in the library. I poured two cups and grabbed the cookies. I was so glad Reyson hadn't found this stash because he had a bit of a sweet tooth and would surely have devoured them all.

"Have you ever heard of someone being doubly cursed, with protection spells woven in? I used your mugwort trick to combine the two potions I would need for both curses, but it just got worse. I don't want to try again in case he's a walking time bomb. I want to get it right when I do it."

She paused, her teacup halfway to her mouth and her pinky extended delicately.

"Do I want to know what he did to the witch?"

"Broke up with her. She showed up at his place of work and started harassing a female colleague. He almost got fired. She didn't take it well and started stalking him. When she finally decided to leave him alone, she left him with a curse."

She held up her hand.

"Say no more. I can already guess the type of curse she laid on him. Those kinds of witches make me sick, though warlocks do those types of things, too. I'm afraid there's no easy solution for this one. You have to go all-out nuclear. You have to write a brand-new spell and potion and just bomb it away. I know you're capable of doing this, Ripley. You were my student for two years, and I know who you studied potions with."

"He's going to be very uncomfortable until then."

"He's just going to have to deal with it. These things take time. I'm not excusing the witch who cursed him, or trying to praise her, but she was quite thorough. It's not going to happen overnight."

I sighed. That's what I was afraid of.

"Thanks."

"Now, I'm out of books to read. Can you recommend something I haven't read yet?"

"Sure, it's not shifters, but we just got a new series about vampires called *Blood Feud*. My downtime isn't what it used to be, so I haven't finished it yet, but I've started it. It's pretty good. We have two copies. Do you want one?"

"You know, I think I do. I'm in the mood for a change. I definitely want it."

I left her to pull the book off the shelf. When I got back, Reyson, Gabriel, and Bram were all waiting at my desk. What the fuck?! Reyson was flirting with Professor Krauss, and she was eating it up. Gabriel was just standing there gazing at her in awe.

"Oh, thank you, Ripley. Your friends are lovely. Remember what I said, dear. Try the jasmine."

Professor Krauss floated off, and I glared at them.

"Is it done?"

It didn't look done. They all looked like they were in a shitty mood. Bram ran his fingers through his hair and sighed, he looked irritated.

"No, it's not. The painting in the vault is just a regular magical painting. It doesn't have Dorian's soul in it. I can't track the painting because I didn't make the contract. The only people who know where the painting really is are Dorian and Talvath. Hopefully, Balthazar and Felix come back and let us know Talvath is at that storage facility, and he's easy to break out."

Just then, my phone rang. Felix didn't have a phone

yet and found the idea a little foul, but Balthazar and I had exchanged numbers.

"Is the painting destroyed?" he asked.

"No. Dorian gave the library a fake painting. What happened at the storage yard?"

"Someone is definitely in there, but there's a blood lock, a shifter guard, and all kinds of nasty magic. Getting in there will *not* be easy."

I had the phone on speaker. We all exchanged dismayed looks. Our plan was royally fucked. They were one step ahead of us this whole time.

AFTERWORD

Thanks for reading this book and enduring the endless dick jokes. If you liked the book, could you leave a review? If you want to keep up to date on new releases, excerpts, or the next book in this series (The Profane world will be a nine-book shared-world series with the museum and the academy), you can join my reader's group.